From the Diary of
Maeve Elliott

New Year's Eve

With the whole Elliott clan present, at midnight my husband announced his impending retirement. Many say that Patrick's a lion and I'm the one woman who can soothe the savage beast. But tonight not even I could stop him from making a mistake. He challenged his children and grandchildren to a battle for the boardroom, to become CEO of Elliott Publication Holdings.

I can still remember my joy when Patrick whisked me away from Ireland to marry and raise this brood. Now as matriarch, that's what I want for my family, for my sons and daughter and grandchildren. Especially for Gannon. That boy has got to learn that work won't keep you warm on a bitter-cold New York night like tonight. That kind of warmth comes only with the love of a woman and a child.

The public thinks the Elliott dynasty stands for riches, for success, for power. But I say it's the love and family. That's the true Elliott legacy. And who knows better than I?

Dear Reader,

Why not make reading Silhouette Desire every month your New Year's resolution? It's a lot easier—and a heck of a lot more enjoyable—than diet or exercise!

We're starting 2006 off with a bang by launching a brand-new continuity: THE ELLIOTTS. The incomparable Leanne Banks gives us a glimpse into the lives of this high-powered Manhattan family, with *Billionaire's Proposition*. More stories about the Elliotts will follow every month throughout the year.

Also launching this month is Kathie DeNosky's trilogy, THE ILLEGITIMATE HEIRS. Three brothers born on the wrong side of the blanket learned they are destined for riches. The drama begins with *Engagement between Enemies*. *USA TODAY* bestselling author Annette Broadrick is back this month with *The Man Means Business*, a boss/secretary book with a tropical setting and a sensual story line.

Rounding out the month are great stories with heroes to suit your every mood. Roxanne St. Claire gives us a bad boy who needs to atone for *The Sins of His Past*. Michelle Celmer gives us a dedicated physical therapist who is not above making a few late-night *House Calls*. And Barbara Dunlop (who is new to Desire) brings us a sexy cowboy whose kiss is as shocking as a *Thunderbolt over Texas*.

Here's to keeping that New Year's resolution!

Melissa Jeglinski

Melissa Jeglinski
Senior Editor

Please address questions and book requests to:
Silhouette Reader Service
U.S.: 3010 Walden Ave., P.O. Box 1325, Buffalo, NY 14269
Canadian: P.O. Box 609, Fort Erie, Ont. L2A 5X3

LEANNE BANKS

Billionaire's Proposition

Published by Silhouette Books
America's Publisher of Contemporary Romance

Special thanks and acknowledgment are given to
Leanne Banks for her contribution to
THE ELLIOTTS series.

 SILHOUETTE BOOKS

ISBN 0-373-76699-8

BILLIONAIRE'S PROPOSITION

Printed in U.S.A.

LEANNE BANKS,

a *USA TODAY* bestselling author of romance and 2002
winner of the prestigious Booksellers' Best Award, lives
in her native Virginia with her husband, son and daughter.
Recognized for both her sensual and humorous writing
with two Career Achievement Awards from *Romantic
Times BOOKclub,* Leanne likes creating a story with a few
grins, a generous kick of sensuality and characters that
hang around after the book is finished. Leanne believes
romance readers are the best readers in the world because
they understand that love is the greatest miracle of all.
Contact Leanne online at leannebbb@aol.com or write to
her at P.O. Box 1442, Midlothian, VA 23113. A SASE for
a reply would be greatly appreciated.

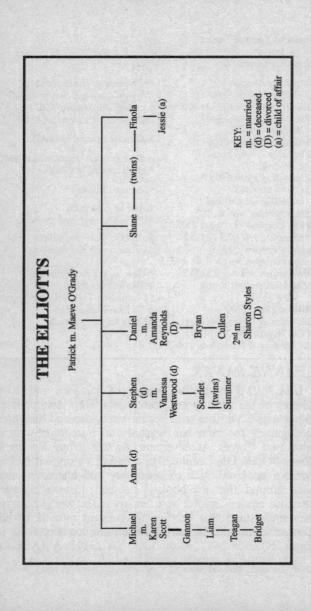

THE ELLIOTTS

Patrick m. Maeve O'Grady

- **Michael** m. Karen Scott
  - Gannon
  - Liam
  - Teagan
  - Bridget
- **Anna** (d)
- **Stephen** (d) m. Vanessa Westwood (d)
  - Scarlet (twins)
  - Summer
- **Daniel** m. Amanda Reynolds (D)
  - Bryan
  - Cullen
  - 2nd m Sharon Styles (D)
- **Shane** ——— (twins) ——— **Finola**
  - Jessie (a)

KEY:
m. = married
(d) = deceased
(D) = divorced
(a) = child of affair

One

"**I** have an announcement to make," Patrick Elliott said to the roomful of Elliotts, interrupting the roar of conversation among the nearly fifteen present for the New Year's Eve celebration. Patrick had stipulated that only family members and spouses attend the gathering.

The announcement must be big news, Gannon Elliott thought as he stood next to his brother Liam. Curious, Gannon studied his grandfather as he held court across the den of the family home in the Hamptons. The Christmas decorations would come down tomorrow, but tonight the lights on the trees twinkled in three of the rooms on this level of the nearly eight-thousand-foot turn-of-the-century home. The house his grandmother had lovingly furnished had provided a haven for the Elliotts through the births and, tragically, through the deaths of children and through the ever-increasing power and wealth of Patrick Elliott and his heirs.

Gannon's Irish-immigrant grandfather might be seventy-seven, but he was still sharp as a razor. He made dominating the magazine-publishing world look like a piece of cake, with magazines that covered everything from serious news to celebrity watching, showbiz and fashion.

"But it's not midnight," cracked Bridget, Gannon's younger sister, in response to their grandfather. "You have the night off, Grandfather. Did you forget it's New Year's Eve?"

Patrick's eyes sparkled as he wagged his finger at her. "How could I forget with you here to remind me?"

Grinning, Bridget dipped her head and lifted her glass in response. Gannon shook his head and took a swallow of whiskey. His brash sister always seemed to be stirring the pot when it came to their grandfather.

Pausing for a moment, Patrick glanced at Maeve, his petite wife of more than fifty years. Patrick might be the workaholic lion who had built a publishing empire, but Maeve was the one woman who could soothe the savage beast.

The love and commitment emanating from both their gazes never failed to humble Gannon, arousing a gnawing sensation in his stomach, a vague dissatisfaction that he refused to explore. He mentally slammed the door on the feeling and watched his grandmother Maeve, love shining in her eyes as she nodded at his grandfather.

Patrick looked back at the family assembled by his invitation. "I've decided to retire."

Gannon nearly dropped his glass of whiskey. He'd

figured the old man was so wedded to his conglomerate that he would spend his last moments on earth making another deal. Murmurs and whispers skittered through the room like mice.

"Holy—"

"Oh my God."

"Do you think he's sick?"

Patrick shook his head and lifted his hand in a quieting motion. "I'm not sick. It's just time. I have to choose a successor, and because all of you have performed so well with the various magazines, the choice is difficult. I've decided the only fair way to choose is to give each of you an opportunity to prove yourself."

"What on earth is he doing now?" Bridget whispered.

"Do you know anything about this?" Gannon asked his brother Liam, who worked for the conglomerate rather than one of the individual magazines. Everyone knew Liam was the closest of any grandchild to Patrick.

Liam shook his head, looking just as stunned as everyone else in the room. "Not a clue."

Like the rest of the family, Gannon knew that the four top magazines were headed by Patrick's sons and daughter. Gannon's own father, Michael, was editor in chief of *Pulse* magazine, a publication known for cutting-edge serious news.

"I will choose from the editors in chief of our most successful magazines. Whichever magazine makes the largest profit proportionally will see its editor in chief take over the reins of Elliott Publication Holdings."

Complete silence followed. A bomb wouldn't have been more effective.

Three seconds passed, and Gannon saw shock cross the faces of his uncles and cousins. He looked across the room at his father, who looked as if he'd been hit on the head with a two-by-four.

Bridget gave a sound of disgust. "This is insane. How can it work? Do you realize that since I work for *Charisma* I'll be working against my own father?"

Liam shrugged. "Is that any worse than pitting brother against brother, brother against sister?"

"Shane against Finola?" Bridget added in disbelief about their aunt and uncle. "They're twins, for Pete's sake. Someone has to talk to Grandfather and make him see reason."

Finola stepped next to Bridget and shook her head at her father. "He won't be changing his mind. He's got that 'till hell freezes over' expression on his face. I've seen it before," she said with a trace of bitterness.

"It's not fair," Bridget said.

Finola had a faraway look in her eyes. "He has his own definition of fairness," she said softly, then seemed to shake out of her split-second reverie. She smiled at Bridget. "I'm glad I have you on my team."

Gannon had never been one to shirk a tough fight and he wouldn't shrink from this one either. "May the best Elliott win," he said to Finola, although he knew the stakes were damn high. "Talk to you later," he said to Bridget, Liam and Finola, then moved toward his father, immediately confident that he would do anything to help his father make their magazine, *Pulse,* the top dog at EPH.

He was an Elliott, born and bred to compete, excel and win. Every Elliott in the room had been raised with the same genes and high expectations. It was in their blood to fight and win. Shrewd as always, his grandfather had known that fact when he'd issued the challenge, Gannon thought. Regardless of who won—and Gannon was damn determined to make sure his father was the winner—Patrick had just assured a banner year of earnings for each magazine and Elliott Publication Holdings.

His uncle Daniel stopped him on the way to his father. "You look like a man with a mission."

"I think we all are," Gannon said wryly and squeezed his uncle's shoulder. "The least he could have done was pass out a year's supply of antacid with this kind of news."

Daniel chuckled and shook his head. "Good luck."

"Same to you," Gannon said and walked the few feet to where his father and mother stood.

Twirling his glass of brandy, his father met Gannon's gaze. "I should have known this earthquake was coming."

"Who could have predicted this?" his mother, the most easygoing person he knew, asked. She met Gannon's gaze and smiled. "I see you've already recovered and are ready for the game."

"It's in my genes," Gannon said with a nod to his father.

"You have some ideas already?" his father asked, clearly pleased.

"Sure do." Gannon knew the first person he wanted on the *Pulse* team: Erika Layven, the woman he broke up with over a year ago.

Erika Layven reviewed the layout for the April issue of *HomeStyle* magazine with a critical eye as she took another sip of instant hot chocolate with marshmallows. Wiggling her sock-clad feet beneath her desk, she studied the spring-flower theme of multicolored roses, sprigs of lavender and cheery pansies. A huge contrast from the gray, bitter-cold January late afternoon she glimpsed outside her fifteenth-story window in Manhattan.

The weather made her feel cold and old. The recent report from her doctor hadn't helped much either. Add to that the New Year's Eve party she'd attended with a forgettable man and the more forgettable kiss at midnight and she could feel downright morose.

If not for the pansies, she told herself and straightened in her chair. She had a bunch of reasons to feel good. As managing editor of Elliott Publication Holdings' new magazine *HomeStyle,* she had the opportunity to help create a vision and make it come true. She had power. She had influence. She had a dream job. If she felt herself missing the rush she'd felt when she'd worked for *Pulse,* she pushed it aside. This was better, she told herself. In this world, she ruled.

A knock sounded at her door and she glanced at the frog clock on her desk. It was after five-thirty on Thursday night. Most employees had left for happy hour.

"Yes?" she called.

"It's Gannon," he said, then unnecessarily added, "Gannon Elliott."

Erika's stomach jumped into her throat and she took a full moment to catch her breath. What did *he* want? Pushing her curly hair from her face, she pulled together her composure. "Come in," she said in as cool a voice as she could manage.

The door opened and Gannon—six-foot-two, black hair, green eyes and killer body—filled the doorway, filled the room. She steeled herself against him and strictly instructed her hormones to behave, her palms to stop sweating and her heart to stop racing.

Idly wishing she'd kept on her boots so she could meet him *almost* eye to eye, she stood in her sock feet behind her desk. "Gannon, what a surprise. What brings you here?"

"Hadn't seen you in a while."

Your choice, she thought but took a different tack. "I've been very busy with *HomeStyle.*"

"So I hear. You're doing a fabulous job."

"Thank you," she said, unable to fight a sliver of gratification. Gannon was tough. He'd never been given to flattery. "It looks like *Pulse* is full of excitement as always."

He nodded. "What did you think of the series we ran on fighting Internet viruses?"

"Excellent," she said. "I loved the day spent with an Internet security soldier. Fascinating." She paused a half beat. "I would have added a fraction more human interest."

His mouth lifted in a half grin. "That's one of the things I always admired about you. You see the good in an article but are always looking for a way to make it better."

"Thank you again," she said, feeling curious. "You still haven't told me why you're here."

He glanced at her bookcase and tilted his head sideways to read a few titles. "How much do you like it here?"

Confused by his attitude, she studied him carefully as he lifted her frog clock from her desk. He wasn't acting normal. Although she wasn't sure what normal was for Gannon. Their relationship had clouded her instincts where he was concerned.

"What's not to like? I get to help rule," she said and smiled.

He glanced up and met her gaze and she felt a mini *kaboom* go off inside her. He chuckled. "That's one way of looking at it." He returned her frog clock to her desk and reached for her mug, lifting it to just below his nose. He smiled. "Hot chocolate with marshmallows. You must not want to stay up tonight."

Erika's stomach twisted and she felt her sense of humor wane. Gannon possessed all kinds of insider information on her because they'd been lovers. A fact she had tried hard to forget during the past year. "A good night's sleep keeps me sharp."

He nodded and paused thoughtfully. "Do you miss *Pulse* at all?"

The blunt question surprised her. "Of course I do," she said. "The fast pace, always being on the cutting edge. There was an adrenaline rush every day."

"And you don't get that here," he concluded.

"*HomeStyle* provides a different kind of satisfaction."

"What if you were given the opportunity to come back to *Pulse* with a promotion and salary increase over last time?" he asked.

Erika was taken off guard again. The prospect of being inside the best newsmagazine in the world provided a potent lure. There was nothing laid-back about *Pulse*. Working for that magazine had demanded the best of her mental and creative energy. It had forced her to grow. She'd been surrounded by brilliant, ambitious people.

And she'd gotten involved with a man who had ruined her for other relationships.

She pushed her hair behind her ear and looked outside the window as she tried to form a response. "It's tempting," she admitted.

"I want you back on the *Pulse* team," Gannon said.

"Tell me what it would take for you to make the move and I'll make it happen."

Erika gaped at him in shock. When the faintest gossip had surfaced about her relationship with Gannon, he'd stopped everything between them cold and had begun to treat her as if she were just another team member. His behavior had knocked her sideways enough that she'd known she couldn't work with him anymore. The position at *HomeStyle* had offered a haven from him, and she was slowly getting over him.

"I need to think about this," she finally managed.

He blinked in surprise and she felt a sliver of satisfaction. Gannon was accustomed to hearing yes, not maybe. She saw his jaw clench and felt another dart of surprise. *What* was going on here?

"That's fair enough. I'll drop by to talk with you tomorrow after work."

"Sorry. Can't do," Erika said. "I have an appointment out of the office at four-thirty. I'm not coming back in."

He gave a slow nod, as if she were trying his patience. "Okay, are you working this weekend?"

"From home." She glanced at her calendar. "Tuesday would be best."

"Monday, after work," he said in a brusque voice that had frightened the life out of more than one intern.

The tone unsettled her enough not to push further. "Monday after work," she confirmed.

"Good. See you then," he said, holding her gaze for a couple of seconds too long. A couple of seconds that sucked the oxygen from her lungs before he turned around and left her office.

Erika immediately sank into her chair and covered her face with her hands. "Damn him," she whispered. He still knocked her sideways. She scowled. She didn't like it. Didn't like it at all.

But part of her response was understandable, she told herself. Preparation was key with Gannon. She absolutely couldn't fly by the seat of her pants with that man.

Erika rubbed her knees and paused for a breath after ten games of one-on-one. She'd had her lunch handed to her during the last six games. Looking at the fourteen-year-old responsible for pounding the living daylights out of her via a basketball, Erika shook her head. "You could show a little pity for the elderly."

Tia Rogers, the pretty but lanky girl with chocolate-brown eyes who Erika was mentoring, shrugged as she walked to the side of the basketball court Erika had reserved for their use. Since she'd been promoted, she got dibs on the EPH gym.

"You ain't old. You just sit on your butt too much in that fancy high-rise office."

"Aren't old," Erika automatically corrected, though at the moment thirty-two seemed over the hill. "Getting paid to sit on your butt isn't all that bad. And I don't just sit on my butt," Erika said. "By the way, how's algebra?"

Tia made a face. "I don't like it."

"What'd you get on your last test?"

"B minus," Tia said.

"It's going up. That's the right direction." Erika patted the girl on the shoulder and scooped up both their coats from the bleachers. A group of men immediately took their place on the basketball court. Erika led the way to the elevator. Tia was quiet on the ride down.

"I need an A," Tia finally said in a glum voice. "I need all As if I'm going to get a scholarship to college."

"You'll get a scholarship," Erika said, waving at the security guard before the two of them stepped out into the cold night.

Tia swore and spit as she stepped outside. "How do you know?"

Erika swallowed a wince. She was supposed to inspire Tia and help polish her mentee's rough edges. Tia, who lived with her aunt because her mother was in prison for repeated drug violations, had been chosen for the mentor program because she worked on the school newspaper. "Ditch the spitting and swearing."

"Everyone else swears and spits," Tia said in a challenging voice.

"Everyone else isn't you. You're different. You have talent, brains, common sense and, most importantly, you have drive."

Tia met her gaze with wide brown eyes filled with hope but tempered with skepticism. It was Erika's job to help give the hope and drive she glimpsed in the young teen a bigger edge in the battle.

"Is that what got you your fancy job in the office you showed me a couple weeks ago? I hear you always need a connection."

Erika exhaled and her breath created a visible vapor trail. "I'm working for a company where most of the executives are related and I'm not part of the family."

Tia smiled. "So you've had to kick some butt, too."

"Metaphorically speaking," she said as an image of Gannon's backside slithered across Erika's brain. She'd had a tough time totally banishing him from her mind since his surprise visit yesterday. She still didn't know what she was going to do about *Pulse*. She lifted her hand to hail a taxi.

"My aunt keeps asking me why you don't have no man."

"Why I don't have a man," Erika corrected.

"S'what I said," Tia said and climbed into the taxi that stopped by the curb.

Erika climbed in beside her and gave the taxi Tia's address. "I don't have a man because—" She broke off. Why didn't she have a man? Because Gannon had ruined her for other men. "Because I fell for someone and he dumped me."

"Wow," Tia said. "Why'd he do that? You're pretty for an older lady. You got it going on."

Erika groaned at the reference to age. "Thanks, I think. Why'd he dump me? I guess he didn't think I was the right woman for him."

Tia swore again. "You should teach him a lesson. Go get you another man. A better man."

"Yeah," Erika said, thinking she'd been trying to do that for a year now.

An hour later Erika walked into the Park Slope brownstone she owned and immediately stepped out of her shoes and into her bunny slippers. She looked down at the pink furry footwear and smiled. They always made her smile.

Making a mental promise to wash the clothes in her gym bag, she left the bag in the hallway and headed for the kitchen as she glanced through her mail. Bills, bills... She paused at the postcard that featured a Caribbean cruise and felt a longing for hot weather, sunshine, an icy margarita and the sound of steel-drum music.

Sighing, she dismissed the mini fantasy and used her remote to turn on the sound of Alicia Keys while she poured herself a glass of red wine. She picked up her phone and listened to her messages.

The first was from one of her best friends, inviting her to visit a trendy new bar. The second was her mother checking on her. Erika bit her lip in response to that. Her mother had called her at a weak moment and Erika had told her too much about the results of her doctor's visit. The third message was from Doug. *Doug the dud,* she added. A nice enough guy. He was just so boring.

The call-waiting beeped as she listened to his message and she automatically picked up. "Hello?"

"Erika, I wondered when I would hear your live voice again. How are you, sweetheart?"

Her mother. Erika winced. "I'm sorry, Mom. I've been very busy at work and I took on a mentoring project with an inner-city teenager. How are you? How's bridge?"

"Your father and I came in second last night. We host tomorrow night. What is this about mentoring an inner-city teenager? Darling, you don't really think that will take the place of having your own child, do you?"

Erika's chest twisted. "No, but it's a good use of my energy right now."

"Honey, if you would just make a little effort and be more open-minded, I know you could find a man in no time. Then you could have both the husband and the baby you want."

Erika squeezed her forehead. "I'll make a deal with you, Mom. I'll go out with two men next week if you stop asking me about this for the next week."

"I'm just thinking of your well-being. You've always wanted children."

"I know."

"You just kept putting it off," her mother added.

"Mom," she said, and Erika couldn't keep the warning note from seeping into her voice.

Her mother sighed. "Okay. Two dates, two men next week. I'll say a prayer and make a wish on a star."

Erika felt her heart soften. Her mother did love her. She just felt the need to interfere sometimes. "I love you. Have fun tomorrow night."

Clicking off the phone, she set it down and smiled, picturing her parents and the house in Indiana she'd left behind when she moved to attend college in the East.

The town of her childhood had often felt sleepy to her, the pace hadn't been fast enough. She'd wanted more excitement, more action, more challenge.

She remembered the smell of the cholesterol-laden, but delicious home-cooked meals that had greeted her every time she returned home, and the scent of chocolate chip cookies every time she left again.

She remembered making crafts with her mother on rainy days and the countless times her mother had sat with Erika while she'd done her homework. Her father had taught her to play basketball and encouraged her to relish her height instead of being afraid of it.

She'd always known she had the best parents in the world. She'd also always known that she would need to leave in order to really fly.

And she'd certainly learned to fly. At least professionally. In the back of her mind, she'd had a mental plan. Graduate from college, get on a career track that would take her to the top and along the way she would squeeze in finding a husband and having a baby.

Before she'd even graduated from college, Erika had wanted a child, but she'd told herself not to get caught in the trap of getting married and having a baby before establishing her career. It was all about discipline, she'd said, but many times she felt a strong longing on rainy days to make crafts with a child of her own, to nurture and love a human being and experience the wonder of helping a little someone become the very best person they could be.

Her work was exciting and rewarding, but part of her remained untouched. Part of her longed for something that work couldn't fulfill.

Sighing, she opened her eyes and pulled a sheet of paper from the wooden file she kept for mail. She glanced at the medical report again and sighed. Endometriosis. That was why she'd had such terrible cramps. That was why her fertility was headed into the toilet. That was why she would consider having a baby without a husband.

Two

At precisely five thirty-one in the afternoon, Erika heard a knock at her office door. Her stomach dipped, but she ignored the sensation. Today she hadn't kicked off her shoes below her desk. Nope, today she wore high-heel boots that brashly flaunted her five-foot-nine-inch height and a black suit with a crisp white blouse. Today she was prepared.

She strode to her door and opened it, spotting Gannon lifting his hand for another knock. He was still too damn tall. She would need stilts to meet him eye to eye. Dressed in a black wool suit with a faint blue stripe, he would leave quivering females in his wake wherever he went—the elevator, his office, the street. Erika imagined women all over the office melting into the carpet.

His green gaze flicked over her, then he looked into her eyes for an assessing second. When he'd taken the time, he'd always been able to read her. Better not to let him see too much, she thought.

"Come in," she said and returned to stand behind her

desk. She liked having a large wooden object between her and Gannon. At that moment she wished her desk was a little bigger, perhaps boat-sized. "How are you?"

"Fine, and you?" he asked, moving the folder he held into his other hand.

"Good, thank you." Pleasantries over. "I've thought about your offer. I loved working at *Pulse*. It was the most challenging and creative job I've ever had. I loved the fast pace. I loved working with such sharp minds." She paused and took a quick breath and reminded herself she was doing this for her sanity. "But I'm very happy and productive where I am right now. I have an excellent rapport with everyone who works for me. It's a warm atmosphere and it works for me."

He remained silent.

Poo. He was going to force her to say *the words*. She would have much preferred doing this via e-mail or fax. "So thank you very much for your wonderful offer. While I'm tempted, I'm going to decline."

He looked at her for a long moment and gave a slow nod. He moved closer to the desk and picked up her half-full mug. "The job you have at *HomeStyle* is like hot chocolate with marshmallows. It's nice. It's comfortable. A few challenges every now and then. You have to choose whether to feature needlepoint or knitting, find new crafts for Valentine's Day, a decor for spring."

Erika felt defensive. "You're right. Making marshmallow bunnies isn't going to rock the world. It's just going to make it a little nicer, a little more comforting."

"As I said, this job is hot chocolate. The problem, Erika, is you had the best whiskey in the world at *Pulse*. You know what it's like to come to work knowing you'll get an adrenaline rush. That the story you tell and the way you tell it *could* rock the world. Underneath the hot chocolate with marshmallows and bunny slippers is a world-rocker. You can fight it all you want, but you and I both know it's in you."

The challenge in his eyes made something inside her sizzle and pop. She hated that he knew her so well. She hated that he'd known her so well and left her so completely, but she wouldn't tell him that was the reason she wouldn't return to *Pulse*.

"I want you to reconsider," he said.

She swallowed a groan. She'd really had to pump herself up for this. "I've given your offer a lot of consideration. You have my answer."

His lips turned up slightly in a grin she'd seen before. A grin that signaled Gannon was in for a battle, determined to win. A grin that scared the life out of her. "Your answer isn't acceptable to me. I want you to reconsider. My father does, too."

Oh great, she thought wryly. Two Elliotts teaming up against her. "I'm very happy here."

"We'll make sure you're happy at *Pulse*." He laid the folder he'd held during their discussion on the desk and flipped it open. "How would you like to do this story?"

Erika saw photos of babies and her heart stopped.

She bent down to look at the copy. "Making the Perfect Baby: The New World of Genetic Manipulation," she read and looked at him.

He smiled. "I knew that would get your attention. You always loved the combination of science and human interest. Cover story with your name on the front. That's the kind of story that could win awards. Rock the world."

Gazing at the photos of the beautiful sweet faces of the babies, she swallowed over the lump in her throat. Did he know how much she wanted a baby? How could he know? They'd never discussed it.

She took a shallow breath and forced herself to smile. "Very tempting, but I've given you my answer."

He paused just a second, as if she'd surprised him. "Okay. You don't mind looking over the story and giving me your thoughts, do you? Think about it and I'll drop by on Wednesday."

The trendy new cocktail bar, the Randy Martini, was packed with twenty- and thirty-something Manhattanites testing the wild, extensive menu of over a hundred martinis. It took two and a half martinis for Erika's best friends, Jessica and Paula, to get Erika to confess what had her so distracted. "I want to have a baby and my gynecologist told me I need to do it soon or maybe not at all."

"That stinks," Jessica said and patted Erika's hand.

"Maybe you could get a dog or a cat," Paula suggested.

Erika shook her head. "I want a baby, not a canine or feline."

Paula lifted her own martini in salute. "You might change your mind when the kid hits puberty or when you start shelling out the green for college."

Erika shook her head again. "Even though I've been career-oriented, I always knew I wanted to have a child."

"You could wait until you find Mr. Right and try adopting, although I hear that can take forever," Jessica said. "Any Mr. Rights on the horizon?"

An image of Gannon slipped into her mind. She immediately stamped it out. "No."

Jessica made a face. "I guess you could go the insemination route."

Paula looked horrified. "Get pregnant without being able to blame it on a man for the rest of your life?"

"It could be fun," Jessica said.

"For whom?" Paula asked. "Erika grows to the size of a beached whale, then gives birth to something that looks like a screaming pink alien."

"You have no maternal instincts," Jessica said. "It could be fun for you and me. We could throw her a shower and go to those labor classes with her. We could even go in the delivery room with her."

"Speak for yourself," Paula said.

"And we could be aunties," Jessica said with a smile. "I'm liking this idea. I'll even go with you to a sperm clinic, Erika."

"I hadn't considered anonymous insemination," Erika said. "I have this fear that they would give me the wrong vial and I'd end up with a crazy man's sperm."

"They probably toss the crazy sperm," Jessica said.

"But how do you know what you're getting?" Erika mused.

"You don't," Paula said. "Unless you do a genetic study or at least get a look at all the guy's siblings and parents…and aunts and uncles and cousins and grandparents."

Erika thought of the Elliotts. Now that was an awesome gene pool. "It would be great if I could choose."

"Yeah," Jessica said as she sipped her drink. "We could start with that blond guy by the bar with the buff bod."

"And what if he's dumb as a bag of hair?" Paula asked.

"We can put intelligence on the list, but that guy looks good enough that he could make millions by being a model and then retire in leisure."

"What list?" Erika asked, feeling a little blurry from the alcohol.

"We're making a list of sperm-donor requirements. Play along," Jessica said firmly. She pulled a pen from her purse and shook the dampness out of a cocktail napkin. "We're doing this for the sake of your future child."

"I would want intelligence," Erika said, allowing herself to be drawn into the ridiculous discussion. "Good looks aren't enough."

"I agree," Paula said. "And no terrible diseases or addictions."

"Excellent points," Erika said.

"You've already got the height factor covered," Jessica said.

"No shrimps," Paula interjected. "He doesn't need to be the height of a pro basketball player, but definitely over six feet, right?"

"Right," Erika agreed. "And a sense of humor. Is that genetic?"

"Lack of it can be," Paula said and waved for the waiter. "Three death-by-chocolate martinis."

"Chocolate?" Erika echoed. "I'm on my third."

"No meal is complete without chocolate," Paula said.

"I didn't think martinis constituted a meal," Erika said.

"Sure they do," she said, pointing to her glass. "Celery's a vegetable, isn't it? Cream cheese inside the olive counts as protein, and appletini provides the fruit."

"Back to the list," Jessica prompted. "Do you have a strong preference for hair or eye color?"

"No back hair," Paula said.

"I'll second that," Erika said, amazed at how much this ridiculous conversation was reducing her stress level. "I prefer dark hair."

"Eye color?"

"Green, if possible." Why not go for the whole she-bang, she thought.

"Okay," Jessica said and nodded at the waiter as he delivered their chocolate martinis. "We have our assignment now. Each of us is to keep our eyes open for a father for Erika's baby. A tall, intelligent man with dark hair and green eyes. Healthy, no addictions. He must have a sense of humor."

"And what are we supposed to do once we find this specimen?" Paula asked.

"That's easy," Jessica said with a scoff. "Ask him to donate some sperm to Erika."

Erika choked on her sip of chocolate martini. "He'll think you're crazy."

Jessica shook her head. "That's why he needs a sense of humor."

The following morning Erika awakened late, feeling as if a truck had run over her. Thank goodness she didn't have any appointments this morning. She couldn't remember the last time she'd had a hangover. Oh, wait, yes she could. It was last year when Gannon had broken up with her. The bad thing about having a mad, passionate affair with her boss was that she hadn't been able to tell a soul, not even Paula or Jessica.

Keeping the secret had intensified everything about her relationship with Gannon. The highs, the lows, the ending. She kept telling herself that if she'd been able to talk with her friends about him, he wouldn't have affected her so much. Unfortunately part of her remained unconvinced.

Her phone rang, the sound of it reverberating painfully in her brain. She snatched it from the cradle. "Hello."

"Erika, this is Cammie. Are you okay?"

"I'm fine," she reassured her. "Since I didn't have any appointments scheduled this morning, I decided to come in a little later."

"That's fine," Cammie said. "Except Gannon Elliott has called twice asking for you."

Darn. "Just tell him I'll get back to him this afternoon."

"I think he wanted you to sit in on a luncheon meeting."

"For what?" Erika asked, immediately feeling suspicious.

"He didn't tell me."

Erika sighed. "I'll call him in a few minutes." Frowning, she turned on her coffeemaker while she jumped in the shower. Skipping the blow-dry, she smoothed on some hair-wax stuff her stylist had given her and pulled her hair into a low ponytail. She applied some makeup, pulled on a don't-mess-with-me black trouser suit and a pair of boots, grabbed her coffee and coat and walked out her door, glowering as she hailed a cab.

As she scooted into the taxi, she called his office number by rote. One more thing to irritate her. She needed to forget him. "Erika Layven, returning Gannon Elliott's call," she said to his assistant.

"I'll put you right through."

"Hello, Erika. I wondered where you were," Gannon said in a deep voice that slid through her like warm whiskey.

"I understand you wanted me to attend a luncheon appointment. My afternoon is crammed. What did you have in mind?"

"We're having a luncheon meeting at *Pulse*. The subject for the article I gave you is on the agenda. Love to have you there. I think your input would be invaluable."

Erika thought again of the article outline he'd left for her. The subject fascinated her. She'd peeked at it at least a half dozen times after he'd left her office. Temptation slid through her like an evil serpent. "I don't know. Like I said, I'm very busy this afternoon."

"You could scoot out after the discussion about the article," he suggested.

He made it too easy. "Okay. As long as you understand that I'm staying at *HomeStyle*."

"Great. I'll see you at noon," he told her.

Erika walked into the *Pulse* meeting room a few minutes early. Furnished with a large wooden table set with seven lunch boxes from a local deli-bakery, the room emitted a let's-get-busy feeling.

"Very nice choice, Lena," Erika said to Gannon's assistant.

Lena, a young married woman who was the mother of twins, beamed. "When Gannon told me you were coming, I made sure there was decent food. Inside the box there's a chicken-salad sandwich, spicy vegetable soup, a fruit cup and a slice of lemon pound cake."

"You're a woman after my own heart. Wouldn't you rather work for me?" Erika joked. "I'm so much easier to please than he is. And I don't bark."

"Who says I bark?" Gannon asked from behind Erika.

She cringed at being caught talking about him at the same time she felt a shot of adrenaline at the sound of his voice. His voice had always affected her that way, sent her heart and hormones off to the races. She definitely needed to rein in her response to him. "Coffee, please," she mouthed to Lena, then turned to face Gannon. "Good morning. Your assistant has arranged a lovely spread for the meeting."

His killer Irish eyes were a bit too sharp for her taste this morning. And why did she always forget how broad his shoulders were?

He glanced at the table, then returned his gaze to Erika. "Yes, she has. She resisted fast food when I told her you were coming."

"Bless you, Lena," Erika said and accepted the piping-hot coffee Gannon's assistant offered her.

"You weren't trying to steal her away from me, were you?"

"Just making her aware of her options," Erika said with a smile.

"Who says I bark?"

"Everyone," she said without batting an eye.

He glanced at her coffee. "Black?"

She nodded and took a sip.

"Hmm. Black coffee…coming in late this morning… Did you have a late night last night?"

"Nope." That was true. She'd come home early and fallen into bed as a result of one too many martinis.

"Out with the deadly duo?" he quizzed, speaking of Jessica and Paula.

She'd revealed far too much of her personal life to him during their affair and she didn't like his reminders. "As a matter of fact, yes. How's your family?" she asked, turning the personal questions on him.

He paused and shook his head. "Same as ever."

"That's about as vague as you can get," she said, studying him.

He leaned closer to her, making her heart jump. "You'll learn more if you rejoin the *Pulse* team," he told her in a low voice as four more people entered the room.

Michael Elliott, editor in chief of *Pulse* and Gannon's father, entered the room and extended his hand to Erika. "Good to have you back. We've missed you."

"It's good to see you, too, Mr. Elliott," she said as she shook his hand.

"Erika, glad you're back," Jim Hensley, chief copy editor, said as he entered with the rest of the department heads.

"Great to see you," Barb said.

Howard gave her a thumbs-up.

The greetings felt good. A couple of minutes passed while Lena provided everyone with coffee and a bottle of water.

Michael called the meeting to order. "Let's get to business. Gannon, you go first."

"I'd like to start with the baby story since Erika tells me she'll need to cut out early. Erika, what are your thoughts?"

"I suggest incorporating several points of view. A scientist, a couple who have chosen their baby's sex, outlining the procedures and costs involved, and a couple who considered choosing their baby's sex but changed their minds. It would be interesting to learn which sex is chosen most frequently. And at-home techniques that do or don't work."

"I like it all," Michael Elliott said. "And you're the one to do it."

Erika blinked. "Excuse me?"

"Since you're moving back to *Pulse*," Gannon's father said, "you should take the lead on this. It's going to be a major story with possibilities for awards. You're perfect for it."

Erika tossed a questioning glare at Gannon.

"That's exactly what I thought," he said. "We have a contact for the scientist, but knowing you, you have your own. You always found the most amazing contacts and got the best quotes."

"Hey," Barb said, "if you keep talking about Erika

like she walks on water, you're going to make the rest of us feel like hacks."

"She does walk on water, doesn't she?" Howard said, wearing a deadpan expression.

Erika glanced at Gannon and felt a sliver of suspicion. This meeting was way more warm and fuzzy than the meetings she remembered from a year ago, and while Michael Elliott gave the occasional pat on the back, he'd never been one for effusive praise.

If Gannon had pulled his father and three of *Pulse*'s top power brokers in on seducing her back to the team, something had to be up. Something she hadn't been told. Something big.

"You guys are too good to me." She glanced at her watch. "Time for me to go back to *HomeStyle* land. It was great seeing all of you."

Gannon stood. "I need a quick word with Erika. How about if everyone starts on lunch?"

"No problem," his father said. "Don't take too long."

Lena handed Erika's lunch box to her. "Don't forget your lunch."

Erika couldn't prevent a smile. "Spoken like a true mom. Thanks." She walked out the door, feeling Gannon directly behind her.

He pulled the door closed and she rounded on him. "There seems to be some confusion."

"What confusion?" he asked, his face revealing nothing.

"Your father, along with other staff members, appears to have the false impression that I'm rejoining *Pulse*."

"Admit it, Erika. You can't resist the baby story. You want to be back on *Pulse* so bad you can taste it."

"The baby story interests me, but it's not enough to bring me back to *Pulse*."

"Then what is?" he asked, surprising her again with his wide-open offer. "We need you on the team more than ever. Name your price."

Three

Gannon allowed Erika thirty hours to think about what he could do to bring her back to *Pulse.* The negotiation process was turning out to be tougher than he'd planned. In the past, although he'd appreciated Erika's originality and adventurous attitude on the professional end, he'd always thought of her as cooperative.

Even at the end of their affair, she hadn't fought him when he'd abruptly broken off with her. He still felt a twinge about it. He'd always been scrupulous in avoiding office affairs. Lord knew his grandfather frowned on anything that bore even a hint of scandal. Gannon knew the reason he'd risen to his present position so quickly was because he'd embraced the Elliott family work ethic by skipping vacation for two years and because he'd built a reputation of integrity.

Erika had been his one slip. Her combination of natural beauty and willingness to take chances and succeed had caught his attention. He'd never met a woman he could talk with more easily. At the same time, he knew about the kick of fire beneath her black suits and businesslike attitude. He'd seen her naked, felt her body against his, felt himself sink inside her, into an oblivion of pleasure.

He felt himself harden at the memory and swore under his breath. He adjusted his tie and opened his office door to find his father on the other side.

His father looked at him quizzically. "Bad time? You headed somewhere?"

"Just wrapping up a little negotiation. What do you need?"

His father gave a short laugh. "Funny. You looked like you were gearing up for battle."

"Nothing I can't handle," Gannon said and shook off a ripple of discomfort.

"I'm knocking off early to take your mother to dinner."

Gannon did a quick mental calculation. "Let's see, it's not your anniversary, her birthday or your birthday. What's the occasion?"

His father frowned at him. "No need for a special occasion," he said but pointed to the slight bulge at his middle. "She's trying to get me to cut out some of my takeout." He lifted his eyebrows. "Having a wife wouldn't be a bad idea for you either."

Gannon shook his head. "I'm married to my job. I'm married to winning the competition so you'll be the new CEO of EPH."

His father smiled and squeezed Gannon's shoulder.

"You're a formidable opponent, Gannon. I'm glad you're on my team."

Even though Gannon was thirty-three years old, he still appreciated a pat on the back from his father. "Wouldn't have it any other way."

"Okay. Don't stay too late or your mother will fuss at me."

"Enjoy your meal and give Mom a hug from me," Gannon said and headed toward the elevators. "Good night." He stepped inside and punched the button for Erika's floor. Seconds later the doors whooshed open and he walked to her office.

Her assistant had already left, so he knocked lightly on her door.

"Come in," she called.

Gannon stepped inside her office and watched her hold up one finger as she talked on the phone. He nodded and pulled the door shut behind him. He approved of the comfortable but businesslike room. Erika's touches of individuality made it interesting without being fussy.

Down deep Gannon felt the drag of fascination with her. She was perfectly groomed, with curves in all the right places. Unashamed of her height, she wore heels without batting an eye. She rarely attempted to tame her riot of long brown curls. Her hair suggested a wild streak, one which he'd experienced intimately.

She hung up the phone and met his gaze. "Sorry. That was the nervous producer of a new decorator makeover show we're featuring."

"You reassured him," Gannon said.

She nodded and lifted her wrist to look pointedly at her watch. "He should be good for fourteen hours. Have a seat."

Good sign, he thought. At least she was willing to talk this time. Unbuttoning his jacket, he pulled the chair closer to her desk and sat down. "What do you want?"

She met his gaze for a long, level moment that ricocheted through his system. "First, what is behind your determination to get me back at *Pulse?* I've been at *HomeStyle* for a year. You didn't make a peep when I left. Why the big rush now?"

"Circumstances have changed. I can tell you why, but I'll need you to keep it confidential," he said.

"Of course," she said.

He knew firsthand that Erika could keep a secret. She'd been as discreet as he had been when they'd been involved. "My grandfather has decided to step down and he has chosen an odd way of determining his successor. The four top magazines of EPH will compete against each other during the next year. The editor in chief of the magazine with the highest increase in sales proportionally will become the new CEO of EPH."

Erika stared at him speechless for a long moment. "Wow," she finally managed and nodded. "So you, of course, are determined to see your father be CEO."

"That's why I'm willing to give you a raise, a promotion and whatever else I'm capable of giving to get you on our team."

She gave a half smile and glanced away. "In that case, this is what I want," she said and opened the folder to the photos for the baby article he'd shared with her days ago.

She wanted the article? This was too easy, he thought with a surge of victory. He leaned back in his seat and waved his hand toward the folder. "We have a deal. The article's all yours."

"I'm not talking about just the article, Gannon. Yes, I want the article. I also want a baby."

Gannon stared at her in confusion. He shook his head. "I couldn't have heard you correctly. You said you wanted a baby?"

"You heard me. I want a baby."

"What does that have to do with me?"

Erika stood. "You have excellent genes. I want them for my child."

The woman had gone insane. Totally, he thought. He shook his head and opened his mouth to tell her she was crazy, but she raised her hand to stop him.

"Just listen. It really won't be that difficult for you. We can sign an agreement. I won't expect financial or any other kind of support. All I want is your sperm. We don't even have to go to bed. You can donate it at a laboratory. I'll even buy the girlie magazine. All I want is your sperm," she repeated.

He gaped at her for a moment of intense silence, then

stood. "You've lost your mind. Why do you want me? Why don't you find some other guy? Get married?" he asked, although the prospect of Erika getting married didn't sit well.

"I told you. You're tall, intelligent, no diseases. Great genes. If I'm going to have a baby, I need to get pregnant soon."

"Why? Plenty of women wait until late in their thirties to get pregnant."

"I can't," she said, and he saw the edge of desperation in her eyes. "My doctor told me I have a condition that affects my fertility and the longer I wait to conceive, the less likely I'll be able to. I've always wanted a child, so I need to do this now."

The strain in her voice made his gut knot. "What about adoption?" he asked.

"I looked into it. It's expensive and takes forever."

Of all the requests he'd expected when he walked into Erika's office, this one didn't even come close. He raked his hand through his hair. "I don't see how—" He broke off when he saw the combination of stubborn determination and desperation on her face. "I'm going to have to think about this."

She nodded. "I understand. Let me know when you decide."

"Would you consider working part-time for *Pulse* while I decide about—" he cleared his throat "—donating my sperm?"

She looked at him for three seconds. "No."

"But I can guarantee an increase in your salary, a promotion over your last tenure with the magazine, increased visibility. How can you turn that down?"

"I want a baby. You won't have to do that much to help me. Your donation is a deal breaker. And I want a contract."

Gannon swallowed an oath. What had happened to sweet Erika during the last year? She'd grown a spine of steel. Lord help him. "I'll get back to you," he said shortly and turned toward the door.

"Thanks, and good night to you, too," she murmured from behind him.

He strode to the elevator, mentally swearing every other step of the way. He punched the elevator button and shook his head. How in hell could he make this kind of deal? He could see the discussion he would hold with his attorney now. If he found out, his grandfather would have a cow.

Gannon had been told by both his father and grandfather that he needed to set an example of unimpeachable discretion and integrity. How could he possibly explain this to his family, let alone the rest of the world? He walked out of the elevator and headed for his office, giving a distracted nod in response to a copy editor's greeting.

Entering his office, he closed the door behind him and loosened his tie as he walked to the window. Staring down at the city lights, he rested his hands on his hips, his mind sorting through a dozen possibilities.

Just because Erika had made a bizarre request didn't mean he didn't still want her on the *Pulse* team. There had to be a way around this.

Seemed like old times, Erika thought as she walked into the quiet cocktail bar miles from the office. She and Gannon had met in countless bars just like this one during their affair. Far from the office, quiet, not trendy. Something inside her twisted at the memory, but she ignored it. She hoped this place made good martinis.

Glancing around, she caught sight of Gannon standing as he waved her toward his booth. She walked toward him feeling a slight jump in her stomach at the sight of him. It was a sin the way the man looked just as good at the end of the day as he did at the beginning. His clean-shaven jaw and the scent of cologne had made her dizzy in morning meetings. She'd found his five-o'clock shadow ruggedly sexy during the evenings they'd worked late. After the first time he'd left her breasts red from the friction of his jaw against her skin, he'd made a point to shave. She remembered how having his passion directed solely at her had made her giddy.

She told herself not to feel that way.

"Thanks for coming," he said, motioning her to the other side of the booth. Ever the gentleman, he took his seat after she did. "How was the traffic?"

"Busy as always. I'm glad I caught my cab before it started to sprinkle."

"I have a hired car tonight. I can give you a ride home if you like."

"I may take you up on that."

"Would you like dinner?" he asked, giving her a menu.

"Maybe an appetizer and a drink," she replied, eyeing the shrimp.

"Appletini still your favorite?" he asked with a grin that was a little too sexy and knowing for her comfort.

She shook her head. "Peach with champagne on top."

He raised his eyebrows. "A change?"

"I've found I like a little fizz," she said.

The waiter approached the table and Gannon gave her order, then his own. "Whiskey," he said. "And buffalo wings. Hot," he added.

"Hope you've got your antacid handy," she said, unable to prevent a grin. "I hear that as people age their stomachs become more sensitive."

He stared at her for a long moment. "Are you suggesting that I'm getting old?"

She shrugged. "None of us is getting younger," she said and switched the subject. "So tell me why you wanted to meet with me."

"I've thought about your requests and I think we can work something out. It may require some modification," he said.

"Such as?" she prompted, her heart picking up. She couldn't believe Gannon would agree to her demand.

After he'd left her office the other day, she'd wondered if she'd been half-crazy to make such a request. But one thing she'd learned was that if a girl didn't ask, a girl wouldn't get.

"Within two weeks I can get a contract from our legal department with the terms of your employment, including your position and the increase in your salary."

"And an office with a window and a door that can be closed," she added.

He gave her a half smile. "My, my, you've gotten much more demanding during the last year."

"It's been a learning year," she told him. A year of learning, hurting and getting over him. She was still working on that last part.

"Good for you." He paused while the waiter served the drinks, then he took a long draw from his whiskey.

Erika took a tiny sip from her martini and told herself there was no reason for her to feel nervous. None at all. She had a perfectly wonderful position and she would be perfectly fine to stay where she was at *HomeStyle*. *Pulse* would be more hectic, more exciting and, with Gannon always around, much more distracting and disturbing.

"Regarding the other matter," he said vaguely in a low voice.

"The donation of your sperm," she clarified.

He took another drink of whiskey. "Yes. I'll have to do that through my personal attorney. My grandfather would implode if he saw anything like this on a company contract."

So Gannon was actually considering her request. She couldn't believe it.

"This would require secrecy. Not discretion. Complete secrecy. I'm sure my attorney can do it, but it won't be done overnight because he's out of the country."

"When is he due to return?" she asked with healthy skepticism.

"Two weeks. He's on a Mediterranean cruise celebrating a second honeymoon."

She took a breath. "So how would we work this? I would start at *Pulse* after he returns?"

Gannon shook his head. "No. I told you *Pulse* is under the gun. I want you to start immediately."

She laughed. "I don't see how. *HomeStyle* will need some sort of transition."

"I've already suggested that Donna Timoni could take your place. You can start work at *Pulse* by the beginning of next week."

Erika blinked at him. Although she agreed that Donna Timoni would be her ideal successor, she wasn't ready to hand over the reins this second. "This is fast."

"Have you forgotten?" he asked with more than a hint of daring in his green eyes. "At *Pulse* the only speeds are fast, faster and fastest."

She nodded, remembering the magazine's mantra. "We don't leave them laughing. We leave them in the dust." She paused and took a sip of her martini. "What about the contracts?"

"Like I said, I can have the company contract for you within a week or two. The personal contract will take a little longer."

"Okay. There's only one other part to this agreement. I can go back anytime."

"It's a deal," he said and met her gaze. "You won't want to go back, Erika. If you're honest with yourself, you'll admit you've missed *Pulse*."

His instincts about her had always gotten under her skin. No man had known her better. No man had been more intuitive about her. In bed or out. She swallowed a sigh. Just because she was getting his sperm didn't mean she was getting his heart or his mind. Or even his body, if he made his deposit at a lab.

Working with him every day would probably drive her mad. She would use all that excess energy to keep looking for the man who could top Gannon Elliott.

The appetizers arrived and they naturally changed the topic of conversation. While she shared her shrimp with Gannon, she asked about his grandmother, Maeve Elliott.

"I've always been fascinated by the story of how your grandfather and grandmother got together," she said.

He offered her a buffalo wing and she shook her head. "The seamstress and the tycoon who stole her away from Ireland."

"How has she put up with your grandfather all these years?"

"He adores her," Gannon said. "And she's a saint. You can't help but love her. She makes up for all the affection Grandfather has such a tough time giving."

"She's the one member of your family I always wanted to meet," Erika said, then quickly realized she should have kept that confession to herself. "It would have been a great feature for *HomeStyle*. Tea with Maeve Elliott."

"Not a bad idea for *Pulse* for a personality-slash-human interest story."

"You're a total thief," she accused.

"Put your loyalties in the right place, Erika. You're on my team now."

His possessive tone sent a shiver of pleasure through her. She remembered when he had made her feel as if she were the most important woman in the world. He tried again, unsuccessfully, to tempt her to eat a buffalo wing and asked about her best girlfriends. He knew about them, but they didn't know about him.

They finished the appetizers and another drink, and Erika glanced at her watch. "Oh my goodness. It's ten o'clock."

He grabbed her wrist. "Nah. Your watch must be wrong."

"Check yours," she said. "Where did the time go?"

He looked at his watch and swore, then met her gaze and held it for a long moment. "We never had any trouble filling the moments."

Her stomach tightened at his reference to their past relationship. She shook her head. "No. We didn't."

His gaze held hers for another moment before he looked away and sighed. It was probably her imagination, but she would have sworn there was just a little longing in that sigh.

"You want a ride?" he asked.

"That would be nice."

After calling for the car, he paid the check and ushered her outside. "There it is," he said, pointing to a black Town Car. "I'll get it," he said to the driver as the man stepped out of the car. He held the door open and Erika slid across the leather bench seat. Gannon followed, closing the door behind him.

"Still in Park Slope?" he asked.

"Yes," she said, immediately aware of his closeness. She smelled a hint of aftershave mixed with whiskey and the combined scents of Italian leather and fine wool. As he gave her Brooklyn address to the driver, she glanced down at his long legs. She knew he'd played soccer in college, but she'd always wanted to play one-on-one with him. She knew he was a ferocious competitor no matter the game.

He touched her shoulder and she looked at him. "Yes?"

"I said you should buckle up," he told her, reaching over her shoulder to pull the strap across her. "Didn't you hear me?"

She smiled. "That second martini must have hit me."

The car swerved, throwing Erika against Gannon's chest. His arms closed around her.

The driver slammed on his brakes and swore. "Sorry, folks," he said.

Her face inches from Gannon's, Erika stared into his green eyes, holding her breath. She felt his gaze move to her lips, burning her with the imprint from his eyes.

"Once for old time's sake?" he asked in a low voice, sliding his hand behind her neck. "We need to get this out of our systems, don't we?"

She could have pulled away. He would have allowed her to refuse.

But she didn't.

Four

Erika held her breath. Her heart seemed to pause, too, as if she'd been waiting for this, for him, for such a long time. Microseconds lasted forever.

Finally his lips touched hers. He increased the pressure and she sighed. He rubbed his mouth sensually over hers and she allowed herself the guilty pleasure of sinking into him. He slid his tongue past her lips and she tasted the cool peppermint candy the waiter had left with the bill.

As he massaged the back of her neck, she leaned into him, wanting more. The sensitive tips of her breasts grazed his hard chest and she swallowed a moan. She hadn't known her body had responded to his so quickly. She was so wrapped up in how he felt that she forgot how he affected her.

He lowered one of his hands to the side of her breast, and her heart stuttered. She wanted him to caress and squeeze her. She wanted his bare hand on her bare breast. An intimate image seared her mind of the two of them, tangled together as close as a man and woman could get.

Gannon deepened the kiss and Erika felt her mind turn like a kaleidoscope. With each turn she grew more dizzy.

The sound of a cough penetrated the roar of arousal in her ears. The cough sounded again. Gannon reluctantly pulled away, his eyes dark, mirroring the same passion that kicked through Erika.

"Uh, excuse me, Mr. Elliott," the driver said. "I didn't want to interrupt, but we've been parked for three minutes now and that policeman across the street keeps pointing at his watch."

Arousal and embarrassment warred for domination inside her. Erika licked her lips, tasting Gannon all over again. Swallowing a groan, she glanced away and covered her eyes to compose herself. She could just guess how worked up she looked. She probably looked as if she would have been willing for Gannon to take her in the backseat, heedless of the driver's presence or the anal policeman across the street.

She adjusted her hair and pulled her coat around her more securely. "Well, thank you for the ride. It was fun catching up over cocktails. I guess I'll be seeing you in the office."

"I'll walk you to the door," he said.

"Not necessary," she said, needing to get away from him so her brain cells would begin working properly. "I don't want you to get a ticket."

"Carl, go ahead and drive around the block once. I'll

be here when you get back," Gannon said and helped her out of the car.

He escorted her to the door, and when they stopped, Erika was reluctant to look at him. She didn't want him to see what she knew was written on her face. "Thanks ag—"

She broke off when she felt his fingers on her chin, lifting it so she would meet his gaze.

"I didn't realize how much I'd missed you," he whispered.

"Well, that's one of us," she said, thinking she'd realized how much she'd missed him every waking minute since they'd broken up.

"I really shouldn't kiss you," he said.

"That's right."

"We're both going to have to keep our relationship professional. We can't let what happened last year happen again," he told her.

"I agree," she said firmly. "So stop looking at me like you want to make love to me against that door."

He sucked in a sharp breath and leaned against her, nudging her against the building. "As long as you stop looking at me like you want me to take you against that door."

"No problem for me," she whispered, her heart pounding in her ears.

"Or me." Immediately he made liars of both of them when he took her mouth again and gave her a kiss that screamed *sex*.

* * *

Four days later Erika sipped another cup of coffee halfway through another fourteen-hour day as she joined the *Pulse* staff meeting.

Michael Elliott sat at the head of the table with Gannon to his right and Teagan, also known as Tag, Michael's youngest son, to his left. Erika gave a quick nod to Gannon but purposely didn't meet his eyes.

After going at it with him in front of her Brooklyn brownstone, she'd decided she needed a strategy if she was going to work for *Pulse*. Number one on the list was to avoid Gannon. Number two was the two-foot rule. Always keep two feet between herself and Gannon.

In this instance, number two was easy to keep because she chose to sit on the opposite side of the room.

"Hi, Erika. Good to see you," Michael said.

"Thank you, Mr. Elliott. Good to see you, too," she said.

"How much longer do you think you'll be dividing your time between *Pulse* and *HomeStyle?*" he asked, ever the hard-edged businessman. "We'd like all your attention here."

"I appreciate that, Mr. Elliott, and trust me, I'll be happy when I can stop bouncing back and forth between the fifteenth and twentieth floors."

Teagan smiled in sympathy. "Feel like a yo-yo?"

"A little, but that will change soon enough."

"When?" Gannon asked.

Erika tensed. She didn't like being put on the spot. Plus Gannon had made it clear that she would be working for his father, not him. Barely glancing at Gannon, she looked at Michael. "I hope to wrap up most of my pressing business with *HomeStyle* within two weeks."

"Good," Michael said, then his lips twitched with humor. "We're just greedy for the edge you're going to give us."

Erika smiled. "You flatter me. Thank you."

"Not really," Teagan said. "If you've got a magic wand in your purse, we'll take that, too."

"We won't need magic," Gannon said.

"As if you wouldn't use it if you had it," Tag retorted. "Everyone knows us Elliotts are a bloodthirsty, competitive lot. You think Liam has forgotten when Bryan broke Liam's arm during a touch football game at the Tides?"

Erika knew that Liam was Tag and Gannon's other brother and that Bryan was one of their many cousins.

"It was an accident," Michael said.

A knock sounded at the door and Michael frowned in displeasure. "Who is it?" he barked.

The door cracked open and Bridget, Michael's daughter, stepped just inside the room. "Sheesh, what a face," Bridget said to her father. "You'd think I interrupted a discussion on the fate of the country." She gave a quick glance around the room and her gaze paused on Erika. Realization crossed Bridget's face. "Oh, not the fate of the country," she corrected. "The fate of EPH. How sneaky that you pulled in Erika Layven. We were looking at her for *Charisma*. Finola will be disappointed. I hope they promised you the moon, Erika, because you're worth it."

Erika couldn't help smiling at Bridget's smart humor. Finola was Michael's sister and she was editor in chief of *Charisma*. Finola also employed Bridget as her photo editor. It must cause Michael endless heartburn knowing his own daughter was working against him. "Close," Erika said, referring to the moon. "Please tell Finola thanks for thinking of me."

Gannon cleared his throat. "Dear sister, what are you doing here?"

Bridget batted her eyes. "You're not happy to see me?"

"Bridget," her father said, clearly ready for the nonsense to end.

"I just wanted to tell you personally that I can't come to dinner tonight. Please tell Mom I'm sorry. Finola wants me to stay late."

Michael nodded. "Your mother will be disappointed," he said.

"I know." She threw him a kiss. "I'll make it up to both of you." She threw a saucy smile at the group. "Good luck."

Michael cracked a smile, pride beaming through his usual hard-nosed attitude. Bridget closed the door behind her and Michael cleared his throat. "Okay, back to work."

An hour later the meeting ended and Erika headed

for the elevator. Just as she hit the button for the fifteenth floor, Gannon appeared and slid inside. "You
want to go up to the executive dining hall so we can talk
about your story more? I had an idea—"

Erika shook her head. "I can't afford the time right
now. I need to look over photos from a shoot of comfortable European homes." She sighed. "That's the closest I'll get to Europe for a while."

"Maybe you can dream up a feature set in Europe,"
Gannon said.

"No time," Erika said again and shrugged. "It's just
cabin fever. I get it every January. The cold temperatures, the gray sky, always having to be inside." She
smiled. "I get anxious for recess."

The elevator doors whooshed open and Gannon followed her to her office. Erika felt a sliver of irritation.
He was distracting and she had no time for distractions
at the moment. She stepped behind her desk. "I wish I
could talk with you right now, but I really can't."

"Okay. You want to meet for a drink after—"

"No," she said and added, "thank you."

He looked at her for a long moment. "Is this about
what happened the other night?"

"You mean the foreplay on my front doorstep?" she
asked, her edginess growing. "You and I have an agreement about your contribution to my little personal project, but we can't let that interfere with our jobs."

"No chance," he said in a chilly voice.

Easy for him, she thought and bit back a scowl. "I

do better with boundaries. Since your father is my superior, it shouldn't be difficult for you and me to limit our interaction."

"That's gonna be tough," he said skeptically. "We're on the same team, and the atmosphere at *Pulse* is intense."

"I know," she said. "But there's always e-mail."

Gannon laughed. "Erika, a big part of the reason I insisted that you join *Pulse* was because of the dynamic you bring to every discussion even if it's not your assigned area. I'm counting on you for that." He stepped closer to her desk and Erika felt her heart rate speed up. "Yes, there's chemistry between us. But it's nothing you and I can't handle."

She bit the inside of her cheek. He made it sound so easy, but for Erika it was the hardest thing in the world not to turn into some sappy puddle of willing woman whenever he looked at her. "Fine," she said. "Limit your time alone with me and always keep two feet away and I think we'll be fine."

"Two feet?" he echoed, staring at her in surprise.

"Minimum," she said crisply. "I'm glad you find it easy to keep business and emotion—or in this case perhaps I should say hormones—separate. But unlike you, I'm mere mortal, carbon-based, and boundaries help me immensely."

"And what about when the time comes for me to make my *contribution* to your little personal project?"

"I thought we agreed you would do that in a lab."

"If you don't change your mind," he said, his mouth stretching upward in a sexual grin that unfairly threatened her knees. And her spine.

"That's pretty arrogant," she told him.

"We'll see. Since you're busy now, I'll stop by tomorrow night," he said and strolled out of the room.

Erika bared her teeth and gave a low growl. The man was so aggravating. What made it worse was that he was right. She hated that. He tempted her, always had. She wished she possessed the magic antidote for his effect on her.

The following day she dropped Gannon a quick e-mail telling him she couldn't meet him due to a mentor meeting, which was the truth. Tia had asked to rearrange their meeting because of a conflicting basketball game.

Erika arranged for a taxi to pick Tia up and met her for a quick bite to eat. Afterward she brought Tia upstairs to the nearly deserted office to show her some of the inner workings of *HomeStyle* magazine.

"It's cool and pretty, but it's kinda boring. I'd rather write an article about something more important than arranging flowers," Tia said.

Erika secretly agreed, but she knew she needed to provide perspective. "Yes, but I've gained new skills by taking this job. I've been one of the top people, so I've learned to make decisions quickly when necessary. It's also given me a better appreciation of how our surroundings or environment can affect our attitudes and emotions."

"Like a cold, rainy day makes you want to skip school," Tia said, skimming her hand over Erika's desk and smiling at the frog clock.

"Not you, of course," Erika said. "You've got the idea. Another example is how a drab room can make you feel tired."

Tia nodded. "My math room needs to be painted. It's dirty beige. I want to go to sleep every time I go to that class."

"Nothing to do with the subject," Erika teased.

Tia shook her head. "No, I'm serious. It's peeling and blah. Everybody skips classes in that room more than any other," she said.

"Then maybe *HomeStyle* could sponsor a classroom makeover," Gannon said from the open doorway. "I couldn't help overhearing you."

Tia looked Gannon over from head to toe, then glanced at Erika with raised eyebrows. "Who's he?"

"Tia Rogers, this is Mr. Gannon Elliott, executive editor of *Pulse* magazine," Erika said. "Mr. Elliott, Tia is teaching me how to be a mentor."

"She's doing pretty good for a new chick," Tia said, accepting Gannon's outstretched hand. "I thought the head dude for EPH was some old guy. You ain't that old."

Erika chuckled. "Patrick Elliott is the CEO of Elliott Publication Holdings. Patrick is Gannon's grandfather."

"Oh," Tia said. "Not to upset Miss Layven, but *Pulse* is way better than *HomeStyle*."

Gannon smiled. "Thank you. I'm partial to it. And Miss Layven will be moving permanently to the *Pulse* team as soon as we can arrange it."

Tia gaped at Erika. "That is just so cool."

"If you want to get a makeover for your math classroom, better start asking now," Gannon said.

Erika looked at him. "You're serious."

"Sure. Decorating, human interest and community service. I may even lift a brush in contribution."

Erika did a double take. "I didn't know you could paint."

He tossed her a dark look. "It's not that difficult."

"But do you have actual personal experience?" she asked in disbelief. After all, Gannon was a billionaire. Why would he need to *paint?*

Gannon nodded. "Yes. Teagan, Liam, Cullen and I painted the boathouse one weekend when we were teenagers. My grandfather thought it would build character."

"Did it?" Erika couldn't resist asking.

"It increased my desire to make good grades so I wouldn't have to paint for a living," he said.

A new story about Gannon's past. Delighted, Erika smiled, feeling as if she'd been given jewelry.

"Grades again," Tia said. "You sound like Miss Layven."

"Good to know we agree on a couple of things," he muttered. "How long are you two planning to be here?"

"We're actually leaving," Erika said. "Hot chocolate, then I'll put Tia in a cab. School night."

Tia wrinkled her nose.

"Mind if I join you?" Gannon asked. "I can offer the use of my car."

"Cool," Tia said. "Is it a limo?"

Gannon's lips twitched in humor. "Sorry, just a chauffeured Town Car."

"That's okay," Tia said. "It might look too pimpin' if we showed up in a limo in my neighborhood."

"You really don't need to do this," Erika said, thinking about the return ride in his hired car, alone with him. How was she going to stick to her two-foot rule in the backseat of his car?

"No problem. We can discuss the classroom make-over and then you and I can talk some *Pulse* possibilities on the return drive."

Erika grudgingly had to admit that Gannon was on his best behavior with Tia. He answered her questions, gently teased her and encouraged her about her studies. He picked up the tab for the hot chocolate and during the drive to Tia's apartment he asked her how she would like to see the room decorated.

"It needs to be a bright color so we'll stay awake," Tia said. "Yellow…"

"Research indicates that babies cry more in rooms painted yellow and people tend to become more emotional," Erika said.

Gannon threw her a questioning glance. "How do you know that about babies?"

Erika shrugged. "Just one of those things I picked

up through *HomeStyle*. Red is a stimulating color, but some studies indicate an association with aggression."

Tia rolled her eyes. "We don't need no more aggression. There's fights every day."

"*Any* more aggression," Erika automatically corrected. "And there *are* fights every day."

"That's what I said," Tia said.

Gannon made an amused choking sound.

"Don't say no right away. But I'd like you to consider pink," Erika said.

"Pink?" Gannon echoed in a combination of disbelief and distaste.

"Put your macho attitude aside for a moment if you can," Erika said.

Tia shook her head. "I can't do pink. The guys would never stop making fun of me. And they would be impossible in the classroom."

"Studies indicate that students perform better in a classroom painted pink. Not only do they perform better but they're happier."

Silence followed.

Gannon gave Erika a considering glance and rubbed his finger over his mouth. Erika told herself to look away from his mouth. Away.

He looked at Tia. "I think you should do some research on how color affects mood and write a very short article. With Miss Layven's approval, *Home-Style* can print your short article within the classroom redo feature. You choose the redo, within reason, based on your research and you get a writing credit."

Tia dropped her jaw. "Me? Write an article for *HomeStyle?* Have *my* name in the magazine? I can't wait to tell my friends."

Erika couldn't help smiling at Tia's excitement.

"Omigod," Tia said. "I mean, it would be much more sweet to be in *Pulse* or *Snap* or *Charisma,*" she said, listing EPH's most successful magazines. "But this is cool, too." She shook her head in disbelief. "My name in a national magazine."

"You'll need to do your research," Erika said.

"I will," Tia agreed.

"And Miss Layven will edit your article. You need to be prepared for rewrites," Gannon said.

"That's okay. I can do that," she said, nodding as the car pulled in front of her apartment building. She looked from Gannon to Erika, then back at Gannon. She reached out and grabbed his hand. "Thank you so much, Mr. Elliott! I won't disappoint you."

She turned to Erika and threw her arms around her. "Miss Layven, you're the best thing that ever happened to me."

Surprised at Tia's emotional display, Erika hesitated a half second before she returned the teen's embrace. Her heart twisted with an odd emotion. "I know you're going to do an awesome job, Tia."

"Yes, I will," Tia said and pulled back, pointing her index finger at Erika. "You can count on me."

Gannon opened the car door and slid out so Tia could climb out of the car. "Bye!" she said and darted for the front door of the apartment.

Erika and Gannon waited until she was safely inside, then Gannon got back into the car and gave Erika's address to the driver.

Her emotions swinging in several different directions at once, Erika didn't say anything for a long moment. A big part of her wished Gannon hadn't been so charming, so generous tonight. It would have been easier for her to not like him. His suggestion to allow Tia to write an article, however, felt like an arrow to her Achilles' heel. In an effort to keep from throwing herself at him, she put her purse on the bench seat between them. She needed a barrier. A steel wall would be best.

She swallowed over a knot of emotion in her throat. "That was brilliant and generous. Thank you. For Tia. For me. For *HomeStyle*…"

"You're welcome," he said. "Now you owe me."

Five

You owe me.

Erika's heart stuttered and she felt her mouth go bone-dry. "Uh, owe you?"

"Yep," he said with a sexy grin playing around the edges of his mouth. "Payback's hell. I want you to play volleyball on Saturday afternoon."

The lascivious thought racing through Erika's mind came to a dead stop. "Volleyball? Excuse me?"

He shrugged. "I know you have athletic ability and you're tall. The family holds a friendly little game where employees from the magazines play each other. We need another woman on the *Pulse* team. We're only allowed one nonfamily stand-in and I have a hard time finding a female with the right height."

Erika didn't know whether to be amused, insulted or peeved. "Is this why you took Tia and me for hot chocolate and promised her that story? That was pretty low."

"Two minutes ago it was brilliant and generous."

"That was before I found out you wanted payment."

"It's not that bad a payment. Think about it. What's the worst that can happen? You sit on a bench for the afternoon."

"Why would I be sitting on a bench?"

"Well, you'd be an alternate, of course," he said.

"Excuse me? I played volleyball in college."

"That's why I chose you."

"To sit on the bench?"

"The guys get a little bloodthirsty," he explained. "It's all in fun, but I wouldn't want you to get hurt."

She shook her head. "So I'm supposed to be the token nonplaying female? If the rest of the female members of your family knew this, they would fry you," Erika said. "Can you imagine what Finola and Bridget would say?"

"Bridget's on Finola's team, so I can't ask her. It puts me in a bad spot. Besides it's *Snap* against *Pulse* this time." He sighed. "Do you remember Athena Wainright?"

Erika vaguely remembered the extremely tall, middle-aged copy editor for *Pulse*. "Yes, why?"

"She moved to Idaho. I need a backup player and I'm surrounded by pygmies."

She studied him, seeing the exasperation mar his handsome face. "I don't remember your being this competitive with your family."

His green gaze turned dark with an edge of sensuality. "When you and I were involved, I didn't want to waste time talking about volleyball games with my family."

Erika felt a quick rush of heat and resisted the urge to lower her window for a cold breeze. "One condition," she told him.

"What is it?"

"You let me play during the first fifteen minutes. If I don't pass muster, then you can put me on the bench."

He paused, then nodded. "Deal," he said.

"Any news on your attorney's return from his honeymoon?"

"Still out of town," he said. "I'll let you know when he gets back." The driver pulled in front of Erika's brownstone. "Let me walk you to your door."

"Absolutely not," she said, grabbing her purse and unlocking her door.

"You don't trust me?" he asked.

Erika didn't answer because the truth was she didn't know who she mistrusted more in a situation that put her in close quarters with Gannon—him or herself.

Gannon put Erika in for all three games. His uncle Daniel and cousin Cullen were clearly out for blood.

Erika spiked the ball just over the net, squeezing out another point for *Pulse*.

Gannon's brother Tag caught his breath. "Good thing you got Erika. It looks like Daniel and Cullen brought in a relative of the Jolly Green Giant," he said of Margo, the six-foot-four-inch woman playing on the opposite team. "What did they say her position at *Snap* is?"

"Temp," Gannon retorted, wiping the perspiration from his face. "If she worked there over a week, I'd be surprised."

"I repeat—good thing you got Erika since Charlie hurt his ankle."

"Yes, it is. My serve," he said, catching the ball as Cullen tossed it to him. The only downside of having Erika on his team was that his gaze and attention frequently dropped to the movement of her tight rear end. It had been tough to keep his eye on the ball when she offered such a tempting view. He knew what she looked like naked. What she felt like. The knowledge brought out primal instincts that didn't have anything to do with volleyball.

Cullen shook the edge of his T-shirt against his chest. "Seems to me Erika isn't officially working for *Pulse* yet, Gannon. I could have sworn I saw her headed for the fifteenth floor instead of the twentieth floor."

"You're just scared," Gannon said, tossing the ball above his head and hitting it hard and fast over the net.

His uncle Daniel smacked it back, directly in Erika's direction. Another woman would have ducked, but not Erika. She hit the ball with her head. Tag rushed forward and sent it across the net.

Cullen spiked the return, but Erika set it up again, this time with her fists. Gannon spiked it just inside the boundary.

Daniel groaned, then chuckled. "Gannon, you act like we're competing for the position of CEO."

"We're not?" Gannon said to his uncle and sent another hard serve over the net. Five minutes later Erika won the last point.

"All right!" Tag gave Gannon a high five and turned to Erika. "You saved our butts."

"That's an exaggeration," she said with a breathless smile. "But you're welcome. I'm glad I played one-on-one last week with the teenager I've been mentoring or I might have faded after the second game."

"Not you," Gannon said, lifting his hand to hers for a high five, then closing his hand around hers for just a moment. Erika's cheeks were pink and her face glowed from exertion. Her curly hair strained to be loosened from the elastic band that kept it from her face. The way she looked now reminded him of how she'd looked when he'd taken her to bed that first time. "How do you manage to look good even when you're sweaty?" he asked in a low voice.

The color of her cheeks deepened and she pulled her hand from his. "Nice try, but you owe me now," she told him quietly.

Gannon wondered what she meant and made a mental note to ask her later.

"Gotta run," Margo said. "Sorry about the loss, Mr. Elliott," she said to Daniel.

"Not your fault. I hate to admit it, but I think they wanted it more. Thanks for coming. Hey, Erika," Daniel called. "I'm sure we could find a place for a woman with your talents at *Snap*."

Gannon felt a quick kick of irritation. "Butt out," he said, stepping in front of Erika.

"Whoa," Cullen returned with a wide grin. "Territorial? You think she can get your father into the CEO office?"

"Who's eating *Pulse*'s dust right now?" Gannon asked, playfully egging on his cousin.

"This was volleyball, wasn't it?" Erika asked. "You are family, aren't you?"

"Yes to both," Daniel said. "But we like to win."

"At everything," Gannon added, extending his hand as his uncle ducked under the net.

"The important battles won't be finished until next year," Daniel reminded him.

"Eleven months and two and a half weeks," he corrected. "But who's counting?"

Daniel and Cullen chuckled. "Can't join you for a beer," Cullen said. "I have plans."

"Me, too," Tag said.

"That gives me an excuse to hit the hot tub and pretend my knees aren't killing me," Daniel said. "See you later. Nice meeting you, Erika."

Gannon grabbed a towel from the sidelines and scrubbed his face. "How about a shower and I take you to dinner as a thank-you for your participation?"

"Is that your way of saying I saved your butt?" Erika asked, resting her hands on her hips.

Gannon shook his head and snapped the towel at her, intentionally missing. "Never. But I'll still take you to dinner."

She held his gaze for a long moment, then sighed. "I don't think it's a good idea."

A ripple of surprise slid through him. "Why?"

She shrugged. "History repeating itself and all that," she said.

"I wasn't asking you to go to bed. Besides, you want to have my baby—"

She lifted her hand. "Wait a minute. I want to have *my* baby. I just want your genes."

His ego took a hit, but he recovered. "If you want my genes, then you must like something about me."

She sighed. "Unfortunately," she muttered and turned away. "I need to go."

He grabbed her arm. "Wait. You said I owed you."

"Right. One more reason you need to give me your genes. I'll see you Monday."

Watching her walk away, he felt the drag of irritation and something else in his gut. He frowned when he figured out the feeling. He still wanted Erika in his bed. She would be disgusted to know that she brought out in him the sexual urge to conquer and occupy.

She tempted the hell out of him, but he needed to keep a lid on his impulses. Since he hadn't been in day-to-day contact with her, he'd thought the chemistry between them had waned, but being around her reminded him of how hot it had been between them. Being around

her left him with a nagging feeling of sexual depri-
vation.

He swore under his breath. Erika made a good point
about history repeating itself. His grandfather had ham-
mered it into his head that he needed to set an example
for his generation of Elliotts. It wasn't as if he was a
randy eighteen-year-old. He'd been able to shelve his
attraction for Erika before. No reason he shouldn't be
able to do it again. He just needed to dive into work as
he always did.

Erika accepted a last-minute dinner invitation from
Jessica and Paula. The three women met at a seafood
restaurant. Paula mentioned Erika's position at EPH
and the host seated them immediately and their cocktails were served in record time.

"That was low," Erika said, taking a sip of her martini and promising to limit herself to one tonight. "He
probably thinks this will earn him a review in one of
our magazines."

"You never know. You may mention this place to the
right person and ta-da," Paula said, glancing at the
menu. "Saturday night and none of us has a date. How
sad is that?"

"Speak for yourself," Jessica said. "My boyfriend is
working."

"Ah, the foot doctor," Paula said. "How is our boy
Bill?"

Jessica smiled. "Podiatrist. Wonderful. But more

importantly, I have a prospective sperm donor for Erika."

Erika choked. "You what?"

"I found a TDH who's smart and has a sense of humor," she said in a singsong voice.

Paula smiled at Jessica's code word for a man who was tall, dark and handsome. "You can tell us all about him after we order," she said as the waiter approached. "I'm starving."

"Me, too. I think I burned a thousand calories playing volleyball today." Erika wondered if she should tell her friends she might have found her own tall, dark and handsome candidate.

Paula made a face. "Sounds sweaty. Why?"

"It was a company thing. Sort of," Erika said, thinking that turning down Gannon's invitation to dinner had been tougher than she'd liked. She'd put herself in an odd situation by asking the most attractive man in the world to donate sperm for her child yet swearing off sex or emotional involvement with him. "Sometimes I wish I were more like a man," she muttered.

"What?" Jessica asked.

"Nothing. I'll take the shrimp special," Erika said to the waiter and closed the menu. The other women placed their orders.

Jessica turned to Erika. "You wish you were more like a man?"

"Just able to detach myself emotionally," Erika explained.

"Like me," Paula said.

"Exactly." Erika smiled.

"Well, you may not need to detach yourself with the guy I've found for you. He's tall, dark, handsome, smart and he's got a sense of humor."

"How did you find him?"

"He's a friend of Bill's," Jessica said. "So we can double after you get to know him."

"Another foot doctor?" Paula said. "Bet he's got a fetish."

"That's not nice," Jessica said. "Bill doesn't have a foot fetish." She turned back to Erika. "This guy, Gerald, is very good-looking, and I've already told him about you."

Erika felt a shot of alarm. "What exactly did you tell him?"

"That you're gorgeous and smart and he should call you."

"You gave him my number? Did you tell him I want his sperm?"

"No, because I think you could want Ger more than his sperm."

Erika's first inclination was to politely decline. This would just complicate her plans with Gannon. He was going to father her child. He'd agreed. They just needed to get the contract signed.

She thought about how much he still affected her and took another sip of her martini. Her problem was that she still let Gannon overwhelm her. What if another man had the potential to make her forget him? Or at least help her get over him? What if Jessica's TDH could do the job? She shouldn't turn down the possibility without checking him out.

"Hey, if all else fails," Paula said, "you might get a decent pedicure out of the guy."

Erika skipped lunch and moved into her new *Pulse* office on Monday afternoon. She struggled with mixed feelings about leaving the *HomeStyle* offices, where comfort and cozy were key.

Pulse was more of a man's world, so if she took the books she'd read on climbing the corporate ladder seriously, she would need to hide her jar of M&M's in her desk drawer along with her hot chocolate mix with mini marshmallows.

She refused, however, to give up her frog clock or her small Tiffany lamp. She deliberately left her lamp turned on while she left to meet one of the couples she was interviewing for her baby article.

By the time she returned to the office, she was starving, but she wanted to type notes from the interview. Submerged in work, she had to force herself to answer the knock at her door.

"Sorry, I'm busy," she called. It didn't matter who it was. She needed to get down these last thoughts.

"Free gourmet food," Gannon called through the door.

Her stomach growled loudly. "Give me two minutes," she said and hurriedly typed some key words and phrases to help jog her memory when she returned to writing the article. She could keep the two-foot rule and eat at the same time. Besides her plans for later in the evening should help keep her from giving in to temptation.

She glanced at her clock, surprised at the time. Seven o'clock. She pulled on her boots and stood, stretching.

"Two minutes are up," Gannon said, opening the door and catching her midstretch. He carried two large boxes and a small box. His dark hair was slightly mussed, his tie discarded and the top of his shirt unbuttoned, giving her a glimpse of his muscular chest. His shirtsleeves were unfastened and pushed up his forearms. She didn't know which was more tempting, the man or the food. "Looks like you and I are the only ones left in the office."

"Really?" she asked, surprised. "What do you have and how did you get it?"

"The food editor received these this afternoon. She told me she's on Atkins and asked me to give them to someone else. It's packed in dry ice and perishable, so we either eat it or toss it."

"I hope it's already cooked," she said.

"I think it's a lot of fresh fruit," he said, opening one of the large cartons. "Help yourself."

"Nice of you to share. I didn't get to eat." She pulled out several containers. "Raw oysters, avocados, chocolate-covered bananas," she said, reading the labels. "What is this?" she asked, pulling out a split of champagne and two glasses.

"Aphrodisiac foods."

Erika pulled her hand away from the box as if it had burned her. She looked at Gannon suspiciously. "Why did the food editor give this to you?" *And why was he sharing it with her?*

"The food editor is Geraldine Kanode. She's sixty-three and was embarrassed as hell but didn't want to throw it away." His lips twitched. "She also said she didn't want to take this stuff home and give her husband any ideas. I can toss it…" He waved the container of chocolate-covered bananas.

Erika's stomach growled again. Hunger won over suspicion. "No, no, no. Wouldn't want it to go to waste." She motioned him over to her desk. "What are you still doing here?"

"An editor's work is never done," he said. "You know that."

She nodded and smiled, happy to put the desk between her and Gannon. "Can't disagree. I'm not big on raw oysters. They're all yours."

"Working on my sperm count?" He shot her a half grin that made her heart clench.

"That wasn't my first thought, but it's not a bad idea, is it?" She pulled out two plastic spoons and some napkins.

Gannon pulled a leather chair closer to her desk and

sat down. "Avocado with basil vinaigrette?" he said, offering the small tub to her.

"Sounds good," she said and took a bite of one of the halves. "Delicious. I wonder what this has to do with aphro—"

"Symbolizes the male testicles," he said and ate an oyster.

Erika swallowed a second bite along with a wave of self-consciousness. "Never thought of that," she said and looked at the avocado. She finished her half and shrugged. "Who would have known?"

"Champagne?" he asked, opening the split of bubbly. At her nod he poured the liquid into each glass and read the attached note. "Says we're supposed to drop a vanilla bean in here."

"Why?"

"Something about a Mexican fertility goddess," he said and took a swallow. "Not bad, but it can't compete with Irish whiskey."

"Why doesn't that surprise me?" She inhaled the aroma of the vanilla and took a sip of the champagne. "Delicious. What's in the little box marked perishable?"

Gannon opened it and looked inside. "Fresh fig."

"Fresh?" Fresh figs were rare.

"Yep, and it's mine," he said, picking up the fruit and gently prying it open. "You know how a fig relates to the theme, don't you?" he asked, nibbling at the pink inner flesh of the fruit.

Feeling a rush of heat, she cleared her throat. Watching him savor the swollen, ripe layers, she couldn't help but visualize… "I can imagine."

"A fig resembles the female—"

"I see," she interrupted before he could finish.

"Genitals," he said and licked his lips.

The expression in his eyes was frankly sexual, making her burn from the inside out. She felt her blood rush to tender places and pool. Her nipples felt achy against her bra. She fought the urge to wiggle in her chair. Why was he taunting her? What was he trying to prove?

She should stop this right now and tell him to take his sex food away. The lure of one food was too great. The fruit of revenge. "I'll take a chocolate-covered banana."

"Phallic symbol," he said, and she felt his gaze linger on her as she took a large, indelicate bite.

"Very good chocolate and the banana is just right. Not too mushy," she said and took another bite. Encouraged by the expression of fascination in his green gaze, she drew her tongue along the length of the chocolate-covered banana.

Gannon's swift intake of breath was music to her ears. Closing her eyes, she took the banana in her mouth. "Mmm. This chocolate is delicious." She opened her eyes. "Wanna bite?"

He audibly swallowed and looked into the box. "I think I'll take the berries," he said. "Strawberry and raspberry." He met her gaze. "Nipple fruit." He lifted a raspberry to his lips and sucked it into his mouth.

A searing memory of his mouth tugging at her nipples while he pumped inside her burned through her mind, stealing her breath. She felt the restlessness between her legs grow. She bit her lip, thinking she was out of her league with Gannon. She always had been.

She needed to back down from the game of sexual chicken. After one more bite, she thought and took the last bite of chocolate-covered banana. She licked her finger and caught him watching her again.

A tempting shot of triumph sizzled through her. At least he was as turned on as she was. He held up two sticks of licorice.

She blinked in surprise. "Licorice. I always thought of it as a kid food," she said and took a bite.

"Chinese use the licorice root for medicine," he said, glancing at the label. "It's supposed to cause love and lust. Especially effective for women."

The bite stuck in her throat. Gannon didn't need all these foods. He was a powerful stimulant all by himself. She swallowed hard and smiled despite the arousal that raged through her like a hungry beast. "Well, I'll have to see if it works." She pointed at her watch. "I'm meeting a TDH for drinks in a half hour."

He frowned. "TDH?"

"Oh, sorry," she said, grabbing her coat and standing. She tossed the remains of their aphrodisiac feast into the box. "TDH is code for tall, dark and handsome."

He stood, staring at her. "You're meeting a man for drinks?"

She nodded. "I am."

His frown deepened. "I thought you wanted me to—" he narrowed his eyes "—give you my sperm."

"I do, but that doesn't mean I have to stop looking for Mr. Right. Thanks again for the snack," she said. "You're a lifesaver."

Six

Gannon looked over Erika's employment contract and glanced at his watch. After five. She would still be in her office. Deciding to deliver the agreement himself, he walked to her office and gave the door a quick rap before entering.

She glanced up from her desk, and he immediately felt a kick in his gut just from meeting her gaze. Closing the door behind him, he strolled toward her and gently tossed the contract onto her desk. "I told you we would have a quick turnaround on this."

She picked up the agreement and scanned it, then met his gaze again. "That *was* fast."

"We can discuss any questions you have about it over dinner," he said.

Her gaze fell away. "Oh, I think I'll look at it first and just ask my questions tomorrow. In the office."

"Afraid to have dinner with me?" he asked. Something about her made him want to get under her skin, make her react to him.

She looked up at him again. "Not afraid. I just want to be careful."

"If you're concerned about gossip, we can—"

She lifted her hand. "We did a lot of hiding last time around."

His chest squeezed at the sliver of hurt that came and went in her eyes. "Our feelings for each other were private. I was determined to keep it that way." He remembered feeling protective almost to the point of selfishness about his time with Erika.

"That didn't quite work out, though, did it," she said more than asked with a wry smile.

"Neither of us was ready for a commitment," he said.

"And that's no different now."

He couldn't disagree. With the competition for the head of EPH at stake, Gannon would be more focused on work than ever. "But you can't deny the chemistry between us."

"Can't deny it exists," she said. "But I learned an important lesson last time. Just because a man's hormones are involved doesn't mean his heart is involved."

"Ouch. You make me sound—" He paused. "Callous."

"No. You're just very practical. Even about your affairs."

"Being practical and up front protects things in the end. If I hadn't been honest with you from the beginning, you wouldn't have wanted to speak to me, let alone come back to *Pulse*."

"I'm not sure your theory is dead-on, particularly about women. But I adopted your practical approach about coming back to *Pulse*. I give you something you want in exchange for getting something I want."

His sperm. Gannon was starting to feel like a prize bull. He knew this wasn't the right time to start trying to persuade her that using his sperm for her baby was an insane idea. He'd given the idea repeated consideration, but he knew what he had to do—stall the sperm contract until Erika came to her senses.

None of this had comforted him last night after he'd done his best to arouse her only to hear she was meeting another man. "How was your TDH last night?"

She appeared to pull a deliberately neutral expression over her face. "He was nice. Very nice."

"Did the aphrodisiacs work?"

"That's not really any of your business," she said.

"It can be. I don't like lighting the fire of a woman to keep another man warm."

She stared at him in silence, then laughed aloud. "That's one of the most ridiculous things you've ever said."

"How so?" he asked, not sure if he felt more irritated with himself or with her.

"I hate to feed your ego, but most of the women in this office fantasize about you. You're too good-looking for the moral fortitude of pretty much the whole female race. Do you really think women don't get worked up over you, then unleash their frustration and passion on some lucky, unsuspecting male?"

He looked at her in disbelief, words eluding him.

She folded her hands together. "So what I'm saying is if you dislike the idea that you're heating a lot of pots when somebody else is getting the meal, you just need to get over it."

He raked his hand through his hair. "No one has ever said anything like that to me."

"It's just the truth."

"You can damn well be sure it hadn't occurred to me."

"Of course it hasn't. You're too busy being your handsome, sexy, workaholic self to notice."

"I'm trying to tell if you're complimenting or insulting me."

"Both and neither. I'm just being practical, like you. Telling you the truth."

Gannon looked into her eyes for a long moment. She'd grown stronger during their time apart. Smarter. More practical. He felt the burn of challenge chafe at him. It was the same feeling he'd given in to last year. Only it seemed even stronger now. Erika had always managed to turn his head and harden his groin as no other woman could. Her combination of mental toughness and hidden emotional softness drew him like a magnet.

Even though he knew getting involved with her could wreak havoc with his family's reputation and hers, he had a tough time depriving himself of going after her. Nothing and no one but his career grabbed his attention as she did. He'd broken the rules with her before and damn if he didn't want to again.

Gannon reined in the impulse to seduce her past her practicality until she was moaning with him inside her. He summoned a businesslike tone and said, "Let me know if you have any questions. I'd like to get the contract signed tomorrow."

"Okay, I'll look it over tonight."

"Good. And by the way, my father wants four representatives from *Pulse* at a cocktail party hosted by the United Nations ambassador from India. It's tomorrow night. You want in or not?"

He saw immediately that she did. In her eyes he saw a dozen lights signifying a dozen feature ideas.

"Yes," she said. "May I bring a guest?"

Gannon paused, feeling a quick, unwelcome spike of an unpleasant emotion he preferred not to examine. "Sure. As long as they can pass a security search. Give the name to my assistant."

The following morning New York City was hit by a nor'easter that brought a foot of snow. EPH allowed employees to leave early as reports of electrical outages and traffic accidents increased throughout the day.

Erika took advantage of the quiet and finished some work on *HomeStyle,* then turned her hand to editing one of the three articles for *Pulse* that had greeted her that morning on her desk.

An e-mail from Gannon's assistant informed her that the cocktail party was cancelled due to the weather, which was probably just as well since she was on the fence about whether she wanted to see Gerald, the TDH podiatrist, again.

When she'd met him for drinks, she'd found him tall, dark and handsome, funny and intelligent, but it seemed that every hour since she'd met him, for some reason unknown to her, her interest had waned.

Making a face, she turned her attention back to the article she was editing. At five o'clock she glanced out the window at the mess of weather and traffic and decided to fix herself a mug of hot chocolate instead of going home yet. She walked through the nearly deserted office to get some water for her coffeemaker, which she didn't use for coffee. On her way back she noticed the door to Gannon's office was ajar and the light was on.

Tempted for a second to say hi, she thought better of it and continued toward her office.

"You're not going to share?"

Gannon's deep voice traveled down the hall to tickle her ears just as she started to turn a corner. She stopped midstride and considered continuing on as if she hadn't heard. Her hesitation decided for her.

Gannon appeared just behind her and the sight of him made her stomach do a little dip. "I know that pot of water isn't for coffee. It's for hot chocolate. You steal the community coffee at work on the rare times when you want it."

"If it's community, I'm not stealing it. And I don't advertise my hot chocolate with marshmallows. I generally confine it to my office."

"You don't have to. We can smell it. There's a blizzard outside. We're the only two people left on the floor and you're not going to share your hot chocolate with me?"

Even though he was joking, she couldn't help feeling like a selfish little beast. "Okay, come on. I have a couple extra packets. What I don't understand is why you want my instant hot chocolate when you could get the real thing in the executive dining room."

"Proximity," he said, joining her as she walked toward her office. "Besides, the executive dining room is closed."

"You could tell your assistant to get it for you."

"Except she's not here. And although she would do what I asked, she'd think I'm a chauvinistic ass if I told her to get hot chocolate for me."

She couldn't help smiling. She poured the water into the coffeemaker and turned it on. "And you're not?"

He tossed her a dark look. "You've met my sister and my aunt Finola. Those two file their teeth on the bones of men who displease them."

Erika laughed. "Looks like you've successfully escaped their fury."

"It can be a tricky challenge. Which mug are you

going to give me? The one with the New York sky-scraper scene?"

His ability to remember many of the little things he'd learned about her during their affair continued to surprise her. After he'd dumped her so easily, she'd decided she must not have been important to him at all. "Sorry. I think a cleaning person broke the skyscraper mug."

A look of trepidation crossed his face. "You're not giving me the PMS mug, are you?"

She laughed again. "No. I have a new one perfect for you to use." She pulled a mug from a box she hadn't unpacked yet. "I received this during a Chinese gift exchange at the *HomeStyle* Christmas party. I realize it's missing a zero, but I think it will do."

He glanced at the mug and gave a cryptic smile. It had a computer-altered image of a million-dollar bill wrapped around it. "I'll take it."

She dumped an envelope of hot chocolate mix into the mug and poured hot water, then stirred with one of the plastic straws she'd taken from the community coffee area. "You may *borrow* the mug," she said. "I'm not giving it to you."

"Thanks. You're growing more territorial in your advanced years," he said, taking the mug.

"Just embracing the boundaries that protect me," she said and fixed her own mug of hot chocolate.

"That sounds like a line from either a shrink or a self-improvement book."

"Paula's psychologist. It clicked for me."

"How about the TDH? Did he click with you?"

"So far," she said, surprised he'd asked and not wanting to discuss it further. She buried her face into her mug and took a sip of hot chocolate.

Silence followed.

"That's all? So far?" he prodded.

She nodded. "Uh-huh. What about you? How's your love life?"

He blinked at her question and looked away. "It's not a priority. I've got my hands full with this competition for the position of CEO of EPH."

"Is that your standard answer?" she couldn't resist asking.

He met her gaze and shook his head, then took a quick drink from his mug. "There was a time when you were intimidated by my position and name."

That was before you ripped out my heart and stomped it under the heel of your Italian loafer. "That was before you tried to guilt me into giving you hot chocolate from my private stash."

"I didn't just try," he said and took another sip from the mug. "I succeeded."

"So you did. Please excuse me while I finish editing this article."

He glanced at her desk. "Which one is it?"

"The one on the growing influence of women in sports," she said.

"I thought that might appeal to your feminist side."

"I suppose," she said. "We've still got a long way to go to catch up with the kinds of salaries men in sports make. But that's a matter of finding a commercial angle and creating a rabid fan base. There are plenty of barriers left to be broken." She paused. "I'd like to see some insets on some of the current barrier-breaking women and include a little personal information with each one."

He grinned and lifted his mug in salute. "It was a good article, but I knew you'd find a way to make it better."

"Thanks." His praise warmed her almost as much as the hot chocolate. Sinking into his green gaze, she caught herself. She might need more than a distance rule with Gannon. A time limit, too. "If you'll excuse me so I can get back to it...."

"You're hinting for me to go."

"Smart man," she said and moved to sit behind her desk.

"Thanks for the hot chocolate, Erika."

"You're welcome." She forced herself to look at her computer screen as he left the room. "I'll get the mug from you another time."

She focused her attention on the article for thirty minutes and then stretched as she glanced at her frog clock. She looked out the window, down to the street below. The traffic appeared lighter. She should be able to catch a train home without fighting the extra riders who usually took a bus or car. Wrapping her scarf around her neck, she pulled on her coat and hat. She grabbed her purse and cut off her lamp and light, then left her office.

She couldn't avoid passing Gannon's office on the way to the elevator. "Night," she called without stopping.

"If you'll wait a minute, I'll give you a ride home."

The offer stopped her in her tracks. Normally she would choose to avoid riding in a vehicle with Gannon because of her two-foot rule. But declining a chauffeur-driven ride home in a toasty-warm vehicle that would deposit her at her front door as opposed to walking two blocks in sleet from the train station would be insane.

"Thank you. I'll wait," she said.

Gannon appeared from his office in a long black wool coat with a cashmere scarf bearing his initials. "Just talked to my driver. He said there are outages all over the place. I'm glad my building has its own emergency generator."

"I don't usually have a problem with losing power. When I do, it only lasts a couple of hours. I can live with that, although I was looking forward to using my electric blanket tonight."

"TDH can't take care of that?" he asked, punching the elevator button.

"I'm sure he could if I invited him," she said, feeling prickly at his repeated references to Ger, even though Gannon didn't know who Ger was. "But the cocktail party was canceled, so he accepted a rain check. Why are you so interested?"

The elevator doors whooshed open and they stepped inside. "Just making conversation. Are you sensitive about discussing your TDH?"

"No," she said but felt as if she wasn't telling the truth. She pushed back. "How's Lydia?"

He did a double take. "Lydia?"

"Yeah," she said. "I think you dated her after you dumped me."

"I didn't dump you," he said.

"Yes, you did," she said. "I can repeat the dump conversation word for word for you if you like. 'Rumors about my involvement with you are getting back to me. I think we need to cool things down. This wouldn't be good for my reputation or yours.'"

They arrived on the ground level and the doors opened. "The car's here. We can finish this discussion later," he said and led the way.

Wind and sleet slapped Erika's face as she saw the driver appear to open the car door. "Good evening, Mr. Elliott. Ma'am."

"Sorry to drag you out in this mess," Gannon said as he waited for Erika to slide into the backseat.

She nearly moaned at the toasty temperature inside. A jazz CD played. Erika wouldn't mind spending the night in such comforting surroundings. Getting a cab would have been nearly impossible, and walking those blocks to her brownstone would have been a freezing pain in the booty.

He turned to Erika. "Did you ever think I ended our

relationship more for you than for me?" he asked in a low voice.

She looked at him in surprise. "No," she said in a quiet but blunt voice. "You told me from the beginning that we had to be discreet because your grandfather frowned heavily on Elliotts getting romantically involved with coworkers."

"Right," Gannon said. "Ever thought whose reputation would suffer most if our relationship had become public?"

She opened her mouth, then closed it. "No," she admitted.

"Who do you think would suffer more? Me? An Elliott? Or you?"

"A non-Elliott," she said. A non-Elliott without a tenth of Gannon's power, let alone his family's power.

"I don't want the press involved in my sex life."

"But what about Lydia?" she asked. "Her name and your name were all over the place after you dumped me."

"It's none of your business, but I was never intimately involved with Lydia. She didn't work for EPH and she loves making the society pages."

"She's quite beautiful. The two of you made a lovely couple," she said in a voice that couldn't hide her resentment.

"You still don't get it, do you?" he asked, shaking his head. "I went out with Lydia after you and I broke up to throw the attention away from you. I learned a long time ago that I didn't want the press commenting on my intimate relationships. On people I care about. So I keep the people I care about out of the limelight. I keep it private."

She looked at him for a long moment while his explanation sank in. Was he saying that he had *cared* about her? That their relationship had meant something to him?

"Since I graduated from college I've had a goal of getting engaged before the press could even guess at the woman I'll marry."

Erika shook her head. "I don't know, Gannon. With your family's high profile, that may be nearly impossible."

Gannon gave a half grin. "Maybe. But remember, nearly impossible is what Elliotts do best."

She couldn't argue with that. Her mind still humming with what he'd said about protecting the women he'd really cared about from the press, she stared out the window. As the driver turned onto her street, Erika noticed that the entire block was dark. No light emanated from the doorway of her brownstone. Her stomach sank.

"Looks like the power outage hit your place," Gannon said.

"Yes, it does," she said and shrugged. "It probably won't last long."

"Probably not," he agreed, and a full silence dangled between them, growing and swelling with each passing second.

"You could come over to my place," he offered.

She immediately rejected the idea for the sake of her sanity, her two-foot rule and her time limit, which she hadn't come up with yet. "That's nice of you but not necessary. I'm sure it won't last long. I've got a little battery-operated TV-radio that my father gave me for Christmas. He even gave me batteries, so I know it works. I have great quilts and snuggly socks."

"I know," he said, his voice holding an undercurrent of sensuality. "I remember."

Erika felt a punch of awareness in her stomach. It hit her so hard she instinctively covered her belly with her hand.

She ignored his response and reached for her door handle as the driver pulled the car to a stop. "Thank you for the ride. It was a treat to dodge mass transit *and* the snow."

"Just curious—why did you accept the offer of a ride when you wouldn't accept the offer to sit out your power outage in my apartment?"

"Well, there are two things you never turn down. A ride home during a snowstorm in a nice, warm vehicle as long as you know you're not riding with a serial killer."

"And the second?"

"A trip to South Florida in the winter."

"But you do turn down the offer of a warm apartment with power while your place is likely to be cold and dark. As long as the offer isn't from a serial killer."

"Yeah. Because in this case the offer is from the Big Bad Wolf." She smiled. "Thanks again. G'night, Gannon."

She stepped outside the car and struggled to maintain her balance and dignity as she trudged toward the door. When she arrived still standing, she turned to wave and received a snowball hit to her shoulder.

The icy splat surprised her. Gannon laughed and she looked up at him as he approached her. "What are you doing?"

"Sorry," he said without an ounce of sincerity. "I was aiming for your back, but you turned."

Peeved, she backed away as he came closer. "That's not even fighting fair. Aiming for my back?"

"Snowball fights are always dirty," he said. "I just wanted to get your attention. You're being stubborn and silly."

"Excuse me?"

"You are. I'm offering you the use of my warm apartment and you'd rather stay in your cold place. It's stubborn and silly." He lifted his hands. "I won't touch you."

His declaration pricked her ego. But it shouldn't, she quickly told herself.

"Unless you beg me to touch you," he added in a sexy, casual voice that should have disarmed her.

But she knew better. She knew how irresistible Gannon could be. She hadn't ever begged him to touch her because he'd always initiated their lovemaking until the breakup. After that, she'd been too wounded to consider approaching him.

"I'm not big on begging," she said.

"Too much pride," he said.

"No. I've never found begging necessary." She turned toward her door.

His hand on her shoulder stopped her, and her heart raced in her chest. "C'mon, Erika. It'll just be for a little while, and my genetically grown gentleman's genes would never allow me to let you freeze in the darkness while I'm warm with a glass of whiskey and watching the New York Knicks."

"Your guilt would spoil the enjoyment of the game," she said, turning back around to face him, unable to resist responding to him.

"Something like that," he said, his gaze holding hers the same way it used to when he'd looked at her as if she was the most fascinating woman in the world and he couldn't get enough of her.

She should run screaming into her cold, dark apartment. Now, she told her feet. Go now.

Her feet, however, didn't budge an inch.

Seven

Gannon could see the argument she was holding with herself flash in her eyes. His gut tightened. One of the things that had always fascinated him about Erika was the way her eyes told stories about what was going on inside her. He had the sense that if he paid attention, he could eventually read her like a book. She was a book he wanted to read again and again.

Breaking up with her had been necessary and he'd been mostly successful in putting her out of his mind, especially after she'd moved to *HomeStyle*. He hadn't second-guessed his decision. Breaking up had been the right thing to do for both of them. When his grandfather, however, had issued the challenge for CEO at New Year's, her image had shot to his mind, front and center.

Professionally Erika possessed a winning combination of drive and human insight. Personally she managed to both comfort and challenge him, something no other woman had done.

"If you don't come back to my place," he said, lifting his hand to brush snowflakes from her hair, "I'll start thinking you can't resist me."

Erika scowled. "You're so full of yourself. Despite the fact that you're loaded and entirely too good-looking, you are not all that and a bag of chips."

"What's not to love?" he asked, taunting a response out of her.

Her face turned serious. "At some point you have to love in order to be lovable."

He felt the punch of her statement in his gut.

"But maybe you just haven't found the right girl yet," she said and smiled. "I'll go to your apartment, but I need to grab a few things first."

"You're going in there in the dark?"

"It won't be the first time," she said and unlocked the door. "Probably won't be the last."

"Wait a minute," he said to Erika, then turned to the driver. "Can you bring me the flashlight you keep in the glove compartment?" he asked and Carl brought it to him. "Take the car around the block if you need to. We'll be a few minutes."

"We?" she asked, glancing back at Gannon in surprise. "You sure you can handle it?"

"I haven't been in your place in a while. I want to see what you've done with it."

"It's not bad," she said, automatically reaching for a light that didn't turn on. "I got some help from a decorator that contributed to *HomeStyle*. But you may not get the whole effect since it's so dark."

"That's okay. I really just wanted to smell it," he said and inhaled the combined scents of peaches, vanilla and sugar cookies.

He felt her gaze on him. "Smell it?"

"Your place always smelled good to me. Sometimes it smelled like cinnamon and apples. Sometimes it smelled like tropical fruit. It always made me want to come in and sit down and stay for a while."

"But not too long," she muttered under her breath. "Candles. You can experience these wonderful scents in your own home with candles."

Before he could interject, she went on as she led the way to the kitchen. He wondered if she was part cat with the way she could see in the dark. "Or since you're filthy rich, you can pay someone else to make your home smell wonderful." She rustled in a cabinet. "Could you shine the light up here, please?"

He illuminated the cabinet and watched as she pulled down instant hot chocolate and another box and a bag from one shelf and some kind of liquor from the upper shelf. "We came in for hot chocolate."

"And Godiva Liqueur," she added. "And a couple of apples and toiletries. If I remember correctly, you don't keep food in your apartment."

"I'm never there, so it goes bad. But I have a full bar."

"Bet you don't have Godiva Liqueur," she said and headed out of the room.

She was right. He didn't.

"Sissy liquor," she called from down the hall.

She'd taken the words from his mouth.

He heard something fall on her bathroom floor. "Oops. Flashlight, please."

He hurried down the hall and found her on the floor groping for her toothbrush. She glanced at him and smiled. "Don't leave home without it." She stood with an assortment of things cradled in one hand and with her other hand reached for his flashlight. "Need to borrow this for a minute. You just wait here."

"Why don't you let me go with you?"

"Because," she said and pulled the flashlight from his hand and left him in the dark.

"Does this mean you're getting a sexy negligee to surprise me?"

"No," she said, and a minute later the light from the flashlight bobbed toward him, signaling her return. She carried a tote bag along with her purse. "I'm ready now."

He wondered what she'd put in her tote. Lord, the woman made him curious about the most mundane things. He took the flashlight and led the way to her door. "If you were stranded on a desert island, what five items would you take?"

"Cell phone."

"Not unless you had satellite coverage."

"Like you," she said.

He turned abruptly and she walked into his chest. "Are you mocking my wealth?"

She looked up at him, and because of the darkness he could only see the suggestion of a glint in her eyes. "Yes."

Something inside him burst into flame and he hadn't even a little bit of a desire to snuff it out. Instead he slid his hand through the back of her hair and tilted her chin upward and lowered his mouth to hers.

Her soft inhalation cranked up the heat. He could taste her excitement on his lips. He rubbed his mouth over hers until she eased open her lips and he could slide his tongue inside. Her mouth hugged his tongue the same way her body would hug him intimately.

He thrust his tongue in and out of her mouth and felt himself grow hard with the sensual motion, with the heady suggestion of having more of her, of feeling her beneath him, wet, hot and ready….

He felt her drag her lips from his, turning her head to the side. "Oh wow," she whispered, her breath uneven. "I thought you said I would have to beg you to touch me."

Gannon forced his sex-muddled mind to clear. "You didn't? I could have sworn I heard you beg. But I haven't broken my promise even if you didn't say anything," he continued, feeling an odd tension build between them. It was about sex and something deeper, something he couldn't name.

She looked up at him, her eyes dark with arousal that ricocheted through him like a wild bullet. "How?"

He cleared his throat. "We're at your place, not mine.

I told you I wouldn't touch you at my apartment unless you begged."

She narrowed her gaze. "Sounds like a technicality. How can I trust you to keep yourself—" She broke off and glanced away. "How can I trust you to keep yourself to yourself at your apartment?"

"You can trust me," he said. "I give you my word." Even if I die from a hard-on that won't quit, he added silently.

An hour and a half later they'd eaten a frozen pizza and she was fixing s'mores in his microwave. A fire blazed in the fireplace and he was sinking into his favorite leather chair with a glass of whiskey. One minor adjustment would complete the picture.

If Erika would strip off her clothes, straddle his lap and kiss him into next week, the evening would be perfect.

Instead she was bundled in an extra sweatshirt, sipping her doctored hot chocolate and positioned too far away from him. It was only three feet, but Gannon knew it might as well be a mile.

"I'm glad you talked me into this," she said, leaning her back against the couch. She lifted her cell phone. "Since I asked my neighbor to give me a call when the power returned, I know it would still be cold and dark at home."

"Feeling grateful?" Gannon asked.

Erika met his gaze and caught his unspoken suggestion. She gave a tiny shake of her head. "Yes. I'll have to bake some brownies for you in a few days."

He swallowed a groan. He didn't want brownies. Why did this woman remind him that he hadn't had sex in a while? Why did she affect him so strongly? She was pretty but not drop-dead gorgeous. She clearly spent a minimal amount of time on her appearance. He was certain that was due to the fact that she had more important things to do.

He just wished she would *do* him into oblivion. Maybe that would get her out of his system. The problem with that theory was that he'd had an affair with her before. He should have gotten enough of her then, especially after the rumors started.

Something about Erika made him want to break all his rules. It was more than the need to get her sexually, although that need was damn strong. He liked just having her in his apartment with him. Her presence calmed and aroused him at the same time. He liked talking with her. He liked the way she didn't take crap from him, yet he could tell she admired him and was attracted to him. She clearly liked his genes, he thought, scowling as he recalled her desire for him to donate his sperm to her. For Pete's sake, this was a complicated situation, the kind he always avoided.

"You didn't ever tell me your five things you'd want on a desert island."

"Oh." She took a sip from her hot chocolate and

thought for a moment. "An iPod. With a battery that never dies."

He chuckled. "Okay. What music?"

"Everything," she said. "Alicia Keys, Seal, some beach tunes to cheer me up when I'm blue."

"For a girl from Indiana, you seem to have a thing for the beach."

"I do. I was landlocked entirely too long. I love the warmth, the sand, the water."

"The hurricanes," he interjected.

"Cynic," she said and gave a sniff. "You don't have to visit during hurricane season."

"Back to your music," he said.

"Some classical music played by a full orchestra, some standards and 'Marshmallow World' by Sammy Davis Jr."

"Sounds eclectic," he said, hiding a grin behind his glass of whiskey. "Two items left."

"Hot chocolate mix with marshmallows. I would be very sad without my hot chocolate and marshmallows. And the complete unabridged collection of Louisa May Alcott."

"No blow-dryer?" he asked.

She shrugged. "Why bother? The humidity would make my hair curly."

"No cosmetics?"

"Some soap would be really nice. Maybe I'd trade soap for the cell phone that doesn't work. What about you? Not that such a thing could ever happen to an Elliott because you, of course, would have a satellite cell phone. Plus a search party would be combing every inch of the planet for you."

"Are you mocking my wealth again?"

"No. Just your family position this time," she said with a sassy smile. "Five things."

"Sports radio with extra batteries."

"Can't do without your Knicks."

"Or Yankees, depending on the season. The complete works of Tolstoy. A bottle of great Irish whiskey. And a woman."

She blinked. "A woman? Who?"

He nodded. "A woman who satisfies my soul and body so much that I don't care if I ever leave the island."

"Tall order," she said, lifting her eyebrows skeptically.

He looked her over and remembered how she'd looked naked, how she'd felt in his arms, the sexy sounds she'd made when they'd made love. She was there. He was here. They were dressed. What a waste. He bit back an oath and took a long swallow of whiskey.

She pulled out his game of Scrabble and he beat her in the first round. She beat him in the second because he couldn't stop thinking about convincing her to play strip Scrabble. Just past midnight the Godiva Liqueur took effect and she began to yawn.

"Hot chocolate with a kick kicking in?" he asked, liking the way she looked with her eyes sleepy and her hair mussed.

"A little. Do you mind if I take your couch tonight?"

"I have a guest room."

She nodded and glanced at the fireplace. "But the fire is so cozy."

"It is," he agreed, wishing he hadn't made the stupid promise not to touch her unless she begged. Inbred cockiness had caused trouble for more than one Elliott.

"You can go to bed if you want," she said.

"No rush. I'll get a pillow and blanket for you." He ambled down the hall in his sock feet and pulled a pillow from the guest bed and a soft, warm blanket from the closet. He returned to find her with her legs folded against her, her arms wrapped around them as she stared into the fire.

"I always wondered why you didn't have a full-time servant. Or several," she mused aloud.

"Privacy," he said. "This is one of the few places I can be totally alone if I want to be. The cleaning lady takes care of everything when I'm not here."

"Phantom help," Erika said with a soft smile.

"Yeah, but she doesn't get a phantom check," he said drily. He watched her expression turn serious, pensive. "What's on your mind?"

"Just wondering."

"Wondering what?" he prodded, joining her on the sofa.

"You said that you keep the people who are important to you out of the press. I'm wondering how many women you've kept out of the press."

He studied her. "Not many."

"Not many is not a number."

"Three," he told her.

She glanced at him in surprise. "I would have expected more."

"You would have been wrong."

"Hmm," she said. "Are any of them still speaking to you?"

"Yes," he said, shooting her a hard look. "My break-ups have always been civil. One of the women has gotten married. The other one lives in France."

"And the third?"

"Is sitting beside me right now," he said, meeting her gaze and feeling a snap of the electricity that sizzled between them.

"Neither of the other women threw a tantrum?"

"No."

"I could have," she confessed. "I was so hurt I wanted to scream and beat my hands against the wall. Throw dishes, expensive crystal with champagne at you, a pie in your face."

He looked at her in surprise. "You're joking. You're one of the most civilized, rational women I know."

"Yeah, well, I guess you could say you don't always bring out my civilized, rational side."

He stared at her, trying to visualize her throwing a temper tantrum, and he shook his head. "You're too mature for that."

Erika sighed. "Maybe. Maybe it's the Godiva Liqueur talking. But you know what they say—there's yin and yang, light and dark."

"If you're passionate in one way, you could be passionate in another," he added.

"Could be," she said and smiled slyly. "Bet I've scared you."

"Not quite," he said, feeling his temperature edge up a degree. He'd always gravitated toward relationships with women he knew he could ultimately control. Last year he'd been able to control his relationship with Erika. He wasn't sure it would be so easy now, and damn if that didn't make him want her more. He swallowed an oath. Where was this self-destructive streak coming from?

He cleared his throat. "I'll hit the sack and let you get some sleep."

"Thanks again," she said. "G'night."

He strolled down the hall, thinking about how much he'd like to strip off her clothes and sink inside her on his sofa. The visual would keep him awake for hours.

Erika awakened early and left a thank-you note along with a packet of hot chocolate for Gannon before she grabbed a cab downstairs. Her feelings for him jerked her from one extreme to the other. She wanted to be with him, craved his attention and knew she was insane to go down that road again. Hadn't she learned her lesson the first time? Playing with Gannon Elliott was like dancing barefoot on hot coals. There was no way she wouldn't get burned.

But oh, it felt so good before the burn singed her. She loved the way he looked at her, teased her and even played Scrabble with her. She knew he wanted her, and that knowledge made her nuts. Gannon was the most desirable man she'd ever met in her life. His desirability coupled with his obviously superior genetics was the reason she wanted him to father her child. Even if the fertilization took place in a tube instead of au naturel.

The problem was that Erika knew from intimate, personal experience that fertilizing au naturel would be so much more enjoyable.

Groaning, she entered her brownstone and told herself to get a grip. Luck finally smiled on her and the power came on within fifteen minutes of her return. She jumped in the shower and got ready for a full workday during which she would be focused on her work and not Gannon.

Her phone rang as she was putting on her mascara. She checked the caller ID before answering. Gerald. Answer it, she told herself. For the sake of your sanity, answer it. She snatched up the phone. "Hello?"

"Hey, Erika, how'd you survive the storm? I was worried about you when I heard about the power outages in your area."

How nice, she thought and felt a sliver of guilt at the same time since she'd ended up spending the whole night with Gannon at his great, warm apartment. "I made it okay. We got our power back. How about you?"

"Didn't ever lose it, thank goodness. I was wondering if I could call in my rain check tonight. I'd like to take you to dinner. It'll have to be a little late, though."

Erika held her breath, swallowing her instinct to refuse. Why did she want to refuse? Gerald was a perfectly eligible TDH. Plus he had great genes to contribute to her baby. "What time were you thinking?"

"Eight o'clock. I know it's late, but I'll try to take you somewhere worth the wait."

Nice again, she thought. "Okay, I'd like that."

"Good. I'll call you later today after I get reservations so you'll know where to meet me."

"Sounds good. Have a good day."

"You, too. I'm looking forward to tonight."

Erika frowned as she hung up. She needed to be looking forward to tonight, too. Maybe if she kept telling herself she was looking forward to seeing Gerald, she would start actually feeling that way. "I'm looking forward to seeing Gerald tonight," she chanted under her breath all the way to work.

She strode from the elevator at the office determined to focus on her work away from Gannon today. That was her best course of action.

No sooner had she taken off her coat and sat at her desk than her phone rang. Erika picked up the receiver.

"Mr. Elliott on line one," her new assistant said.

"Which Mr. Elliott?" Erika asked.

"Oh. Mr. Michael Elliott."

"Put him through please." Erika waited a half second. "Erika Layven. How can I help you, Mr. Elliott?"

"You can call me Michael. You may be calling me something else by the end of the day."

Erika heard exasperation in his voice. "What's the problem?"

"We have two feature articles that have to go to print, but they're disasters. I want you and Gannon to take care of them today."

Erika blinked. "Gannon?" she echoed, hearing a flushing sound as she saw her time and distance rules go straight down the toilet.

"Yeah. I hope you didn't have anything else planned today."

"Of course I had plans, but this sounds much more important. I can reschedule."

"Good. I've already told Gannon. You can work from his office."

"Yes, sir. 'Bye for now," she said and hung up, feeling a twinge of suspicion. Had Gannon set this up with his father to force her to be with him? She shook her head. She was being paranoid or maybe placing too much importance on herself. Gannon didn't have to resort to tricks to get a woman to be with him. Including her, she thought with a scowl. Grabbing her pen and a notepad, she headed for his office.

His assistant waved her inside.

Gannon looked up from his desk, which was uncharacteristically covered with papers and photos.

"How did this happen?" she asked.

"Current events. Breaking stories. Fill-in reporter,

new photographer." He shook his head in disgust. "The good news is the photographer took lots of shots, so we should be able to find something."

"Okay," she said, moving to his desk. "Tell me where you want me to start."

Eight

Erika and Gannon worked nonstop through lunch on the features, rewriting and editing. Erika made phone calls to obtain clarification. Gannon sent the photos they selected to their photo editor.

The time passed like lightning. If she thought about the way they worked together—as if she were one hand and he were the other—then it might have freaked her out. But they were too busy.

With her focus on the feature articles, she shouldn't have noticed him too much, but she did. She inhaled his aftershave and wanted to drown in it. He raked his fingers through his hair and she wanted to touch his hair. Once, his hand grazed hers and she felt a thrill race through her. She met his gaze and what she saw there stopped her heart.

As if both of them knew they couldn't let down their guard, they both looked away and forged on. By the end of the day, though, she couldn't help staring at his mouth when he talked.

At six-thirty, when they finished what had initially looked like mission impossible, she felt giddy.

Gannon sank into his chair and pulled his tie off. He'd loosened it hours ago. He met her gaze and chuckled. "Cheers to us."

She smiled in return. "Cheers to us. All we need is some champagne."

He lifted his hand. "I have some," he said and rose toward a minibar on the other side of his large office. Underneath the cherrywood bar he opened a small refrigerator and pulled out a chilled bottle of champagne. "Cristal."

She gaped at the bottle, then at him. "That's a little extravagant, isn't it?"

"Are you saying we don't deserve it?" he asked, unwrapping the foil. He grabbed a towel from beneath the counter and popped the cork.

"I guess it's too late to debate now." She stood. "Do you have glasses?"

He tilted his head behind him. "Lower left cabinet."

Erika walked to the cabinet and pulled out two crystal flutes. "These are beautiful. They look like Waterford."

"My mother gave them to me. Hinting," he said, moving toward her and pouring the sparkling wine into the glasses she held. "Have a seat," he said, pointing to the chairs on the other side of his desk.

Erika sank into her chair while Gannon sat next to her. "To conquering the mission impossible," she said, lifting her glass, enjoying his mussed look and the hint of a five-o'clock shadow on his jaw. She liked him when he looked a little rough around the edges. She also liked him when he was wearing a black suit. Then again, she really liked him with just a sheet or nothing at all.

He clicked his glass against hers. "To our friendship," he said.

She took a sip of the wine and then another. "Very good, of course."

"Very good."

"So what was your mother hinting about?"

"Me settling down and getting married."

"Ah. What did you tell her?"

"Same thing I always tell her. When the time and the woman are right."

She took another sip to cover the odd mix of feelings inside her. "I get some of the same thing from my mother."

"What do you tell her?"

"I change the subject and ask how her bridge game is," she said, and thought about the baby contract that Gannon hadn't produced. She told herself to be a little more patient.

"That's pretty good. I'll have to remember it for future reference." He topped off her glass. "Drink up. We should finish this."

"And end up with a champagne headache? I don't know. But maybe it's worth it if it's Cristal," she said, feeling a conspiratorial thrill as she let herself sink into his gaze. She took another few sips and felt a flush of heat. "Whew. With no lunch, this is going straight to my head."

"I can take care of that," he said in a voice that reminded her that he could take care of her in a lot of ways.

Feeling a twist of flat-out lust form in her belly, she closed her eyes and took another long sip. "Oh, what a day. A blur. Do you think your father will be happy with what we did?"

"Ecstatic," Gannon corrected. "In his way."

She smiled at his dry tone and opened her eyes. "He's not the kind to jump up and down very often, is he?"

"No, but he always makes it clear if he's pleased or not."

"And he's almost always pleased with you," she ventured.

"There have been a few times that I set him off, but I'm the oldest."

She understood because she was the oldest in her family. "The bar is higher."

Gannon nodded and lifted his hand to her cheek. "What about you?"

She should move away, she told herself. She was breaking both the time and distance rules, but she liked the way that one finger of his felt on her skin. The slow movement was mesmerizing. "I'm the oldest, too, but

I'm lucky. I don't work for my mother or father. I live in a different state. At the same time, you can take the girl out of Indiana, but you can't take Indiana out of the girl."

He smiled. "Soft heart under the black suit, hot chocolate. Do you miss your parents?"

She nodded. "Sometimes, but I think a little distance can be a good thing."

"Can't disagree."

"Yet you stay."

He shrugged. "I never considered anything else. I never really wanted anything else."

"Never? You never had a rebellious moment as a teenager or as a college kid?"

"Okay," he relented. "So there was a week or two when I seriously considered becoming a fly fisherman's guide in Montana."

She laughed. "I'm trying to picture you in rubber waders instead of a Brooks Brothers suit."

He moved his hand to her mouth and rubbed his thumb over her bottom lip. "Are you mocking me again? There was also that summer in high school when I was determined to play in a garage band."

Surprise raced through her. "Oh, I never knew. You never mentioned that before when we—" She broke off. "When we were involved. There's still a lot I don't know about you."

"You don't sound happy about that," he murmured, his gaze lingering on her mouth.

She wasn't, and the knowledge irritated her. "Not much I can do about it, is there?"

"You can do more than you think you can," he said and leaned back to toss back the rest of his champagne.

What an obscure comment, she thought, watching the muscles of his throat as he swallowed. She remembered kissing him there on his throat and hearing him groan in pleasure. The sounds he'd made when they'd made love had made her crazy to please him.

He tilted the bottle of champagne and filled his glass and topped off hers again. "Almost done." Meeting her gaze, he leaned closer. Then closer. So close her vision blurred.

"I'm going to kiss you."

"I didn't beg," she said in the only protest she could muster. She hadn't begged. Not aloud anyway.

"We're not in my apartment," he said and lowered his mouth to hers.

All the breath left her lungs. He moved his mouth over hers, caressing, exploring. His tongue slipped over her lips and she instinctively opened, letting him in.

He made a ghost of a groan that melted her thighs and turned her to liquid. He pulled back slightly. "Take a drink of champagne," he told her. "I want to taste it on your mouth."

Oooooh, wow. With a not-so-steady hand she lifted the flute and took a sip.

He slid his hand underneath her jaw and lowered his mouth again, slipping his tongue over her mouth and then over her tongue.

The kiss went on and on and she felt as if she'd been injected with a drug that made her move in slow motion. Nothing moved quickly except her heart. She felt the flute lifted from her hand.

The kiss turned deeper and Gannon pulled her from her chair onto his lap. A sliver of caution dented the thick aura of desire infusing her brain. "Is this a good idea?" she managed.

"We're just kissing," he said.

But her body wanted more, she thought. A lot more. He slid his hand around the nape of her neck and deepened the kiss, his tongue thrusting inside her mouth.

Almost of their own accord her hands went to his hair. His groan of pleasure rewarded her and she felt his hands on the sides of her breasts. Her nipples immediately peaked against her bra. One, two, three seconds passed and he touched her nipples.

The sensation sent a ricochet of tension down between her legs, where she felt wet and swollen.

"Do you want more?" he whispered.

The forbidden offer tantalized her unbearably. "How can I possibly think straight with the way you're touching me?"

"Is that good or bad?"

"Both," she muttered, biting her lip as he continued to rub his thumbs over her tender nipples.

"Tell me you want me to stop," he said, stopping the sensual movement.

So she was going to have to be a big girl after all. Responsible. She didn't want to think. She just wanted to feel him, every way, everywhere. She closed her eyes. "I can't say that I want you to stop," she admitted in a low voice.

He tugged her mouth back to his and took a long draw from her lips as if she were a drink he couldn't get enough of. At what felt like the speed of light he unbuttoned her blouse and unfastened her bra. With restless fingers she unfastened his shirt and pushed it down his arms, but he wore a T-shirt underneath.

Frustration bubbled from her throat. "Not fair," she said.

He quickly obliged her by removing his undershirt. She slid her fingers over his pecs and down his torso, thrilled by his quick intake of breath when her fingers dipped to his waistband.

He buried his face in her breasts, sliding one of her nipples into his mouth. The way he tugged on her nipple sent her temperature soaring and tightened the empty ache inside her. She shifted restlessly on his lap, sliding against his hard arousal.

He gave a groan that mixed frustration and pleasure. "You get me so—" He broke off and stood her between his legs, pulling down her stockings and the skirt she wore. She'd ditched her boots late afternoon in the middle of their intense work session.

His gaze dark with the same need she felt, he pulled

a condom from his pocket, unfastened his belt and shoved down his slacks and briefs. Sinking down onto the chair, he pulled her onto his lap.

He kissed her while his fingers searched and found her sweet spot. "Wet and good," he murmured in approval. His tongue stroked hers while his fingers caressed her intimately.

Erika got so hot she could barely breathe. Anticipation warred with anxiousness. "I want you inside me," she whispered to him. Then more to herself, "This is insane," she said, overwhelmed by the need to be with him, by the need to be as close to him as humanly possible.

Gannon lifted her hips over him and she slid down his shaft, taking him inside her. The way he filled her took her breath away.

He shuddered. "You have no idea how good…"

She lifted her hips and slid down him again, the friction stimulating all her most intimate nerve endings. "Oh, I think I have an idea."

And the rhythm began. He thrust upward when she rippled down over him. He drew her breasts to his mouth, sucking her nipple while he thrust inside her. The dual sensations made her crazy.

He slid his hand between them and stroked her sweet spot, and Erika felt an explosion of pleasure kicking through her blood like a current coming in fits and starts. He continued to move and she felt herself clench in a mind-blowing climax.

She heard him mutter something that was either an oath or a prayer. Or both. And he rocked his hips upward, thrusting, his body arched in release.

Squeezing her bottom, he swore under his breath. "Oh damn, that was amazing." He met her gaze with eyes dark with arousal and fulfillment. "You're incredible. Just—"

A knock sounded at the door. Shock raced through her. Someone might as well have thrown a bucket of water on Erika. "Oh no—"

He covered her lips with one finger and shook his head. Another knock sounded.

"Mr. Elliott? Cleaning service is here to take care of your office."

"Give me about fifteen minutes, thank you. I'm finishing a project."

Recriminations immediately filled Erika's head. What in the world was she doing? Had she learned nothing? She'd gotten involved with Gannon before and he'd hurt her so much she couldn't feel anything at all for another man.

This was even worse. They'd never gone this far in the office.

Bitter regret filling her throat, she struggled to climb off his lap, stumbling as she tried to stand.

Gannon stood and steadied her. "You okay?"

She could feel him studying her face and she refused to meet his gaze. "I could probably be better. Getting dressed wouldn't hurt."

He moved to lock the door. "It's okay. No one walked in on us."

"But they could have," she said, jerking on her clothes. "I'm in here bonking the boss and—"

"I'm not technically your boss," Gannon said. "I made sure of that when you returned to *Pulse*."

She sent him a withering glance. "That could have been anyone behind that door. And what if they hadn't knocked?"

"Everyone knocks on my door before entering."

"What about your father? What about one of your brothers or your sister? Or one of your thousands of cousins?" She tried to keep the hysteria from her voice.

He pulled up his pants and fastened them. She noticed it took him about one-tenth the time to pull himself together, while she was still dressing herself with hands that refused to steady themselves.

She struggled with the zipper on her boots and he brushed her hand away. "You need to calm down, Erika. Nothing happened. I would protect you. This thing between us…" he said and shrugged. "We just got carried away. We need to keep it private."

"I'm not sure we should keep it at all," she told him. "I already bought the T-shirt for this ride one time."

"But you want my baby," he said, meeting her gaze dead-on.

Her throat closed up and she looked away. "I want your genes. Otherwise you and I know it's not the right time or I'm not the right woman."

Silence followed, swelling between them, creating an unbearable tension inside Erika.

"Do we really know that?" he asked.

His question made her heart stop. It gave her a crazy kind of hope that she didn't want to buy into for her sanity and emotional safety. "We know it's not the right time. And if I were the right woman—the really right woman—then any time would be the right time." She successfully pulled up the zipper on her other boot.

"Erika," he said, putting his hand over hers.

She closed her eyes at the strong tug she felt, the wanting to be with him. "No, Gannon, for you this is just about the crazy chemistry between us and some amazing hot sex. And I'm hardwired differently." She glanced at the clock. Seven-fifteen. Her head clearing, she felt a nudge from her brain. What—

Remembering her late date with Gerald, she swore and began to gather the rest of her belongings. "Oh, great. Just great."

"What is it?"

"I have a dinner date in forty-five minutes."

Gannon went completely silent.

"You're not really going to meet him after we—"

She bit her lip and waved her hand. "I'll handle it. I'll take care of it. I'll, uh—" She swallowed over the terrible distraught lump in her throat. "I guess I'll see you Monday."

He reached for her and she stumbled backward. "No. Please don't touch me right now. I need to leave."

Nine

"Yes, Jessica, I had to cancel the dinner date with Gerald. I'm sorry, but I just couldn't make it. Something happened at work at the last minute." Something *stupid* happened at the last minute and she'd bashed herself the entire weekend for letting Gannon *happen* to her again. *In his office.*

Erika rolled her eyes at herself in disgust. The one good thing she could say about this Monday morning was that she hadn't crossed paths with the human object of her insanity.

"But you'll go out with him some other time, won't you?" Jessica asked. "I had to work to get this guy to do a blind date, Erika. You need to take advantage of this opportunity. He's a doctor."

Erika couldn't muster any enthusiasm about going out with Gerald and she feared that every time she looked at him, she'd be reminded of the reason she'd broken the date with him and subsequently reminded of what an idiot she'd been.

"I don't know, Jessica. I've just made a big change at work and it's going to be very demanding and—"

"Oh, Erika, don't pull the work excuse. Gerald is already thinking you're not interested. And really what's not to like about him? He's TDH with brains, a sense of humor—"

The light for her second line began to flash. "I know, Jessica, but—"

She heard a tap on her door, and her assistant poked her head inside. "Sorry to bother you, but a woman on the line said something about you being her niece's mentor and she sounded upset."

Erika felt her chest constrict with concern. "Jessica, I gotta go. I'll call you back when I can." She switched lines. "Erika Layven."

"Miss Layven, Tia's been hit by a truck," a woman said in a broken voice. "She won't be able to meet you."

Erika's heart stopped. "Omigod, what happened? Where are you?"

"It happened this morning on her way to school. I'm at the emergency room. I don't know what's going to happen. No one will tell me anything."

"Tell me where you are and I'll be there as soon as I can."

Gannon learned Erika wasn't in the office when he sent his assistant to deliver a feature article proposal to her. "How long will she be out?" he asked, wondering at the reason for her absence.

His assistant shrugged. "I'm not sure, but Rose said she thought she might not be back in until tomorrow."

He nodded, feeling a prickle of concern. Erika rarely missed work for any reason. After a meeting with a monthly columnist, he gave in to his curiosity and dropped by Erika's office.

"I'd like to get Erika's input on a feature proposal. Do you know when she'll be back in?" he asked Erika's assistant.

Rose shook her head. "No. When she left for the E.R., she told me to hold her messages and she'd check in at the end of the day if she could."

Alarm shot through him. "E.R.?"

"I'm a little sketchy on the relationships, but someone named Tia was apparently hit by a truck and was taken to a hospital."

Gannon recalled that Tia was the young teen Erika had been mentoring. He shook his head. "Do you know her condition?"

Rose shook her head sadly. "No, but how can it be anything but bad?"

Gannon frowned. "Did she mention which hospital?"

"Yes, I have it here somewhere," she said, rustling through some papers on her desk. "Here it is. St. Joseph's."

"Thanks," he said and tucked the information in his mind.

He went back to his office and sat down in his chair,

trying not to think of how frantic Erika must be. He could think of nothing else. Picking up his phone, he dialed her cell. No answer. His gut twisted. Not a good sign.

But not his problem, the pragmatic side of his brain reminded him. He clicked the mouse for his computer to check his schedule. He had a full plate of his own today.

Tia's aunt Brenda couldn't handle the sight of the blood from her niece's injuries, so Erika sat with Tia until she was taken into surgery. She alternately paced the waiting room and gave a hug of reassurance to Tia's aunt.

"I should have watched out for her better. I was in a hurry to get Jason to day care. I overslept, so we were all running late."

Erika put her arm around the young woman's shoulders. "You've got to stop blaming yourself. You couldn't have stopped that truck driver. You heard the officer. The guy was drunk," Erika said, still furious at the cause of the accident and shaken by Tia's close call.

"I just hope they can fix her. She's such a sweet girl. Smart. She deserves so much more."

"You do more than you know." Erika tried to reassure the woman at the same time she was worried.

"How is Tia?" a male voice asked from behind her.

Gannon's voice, she thought. It couldn't be. She needed to drink some water or eat something. She had to be imagining things.

"Erika," the voice persisted.

She glanced over her shoulder and was shocked to see Gannon in front of her. "Gannon?"

"Your assistant told me where you were. I thought I should check on you."

Still unable to believe her eyes, she glanced at her watch. "It's three o'clock. You left work early? You never leave work early." She shook her head, incredulous.

"This sounded serious. I thought I should come by."

Erika was too surprised to know what to think. The concern in his eyes touched her and took her completely off guard.

"Who's he?" Brenda asked.

"Oh, I'm sorry," Erika said, refocusing. "Brenda Rogers, Tia's aunt, this is my, uh— This is Gannon Elliott. I work with him."

Brenda wrinkled her brow as if his name was familiar. "Elliott. Where have I heard that before?"

Where haven't you? Erika thought. "The Elliotts are involved in several publishing ventures."

Gannon extended his hand. "I'm so sorry about your niece."

"I've been a wreck all morning, but Erika here has been a lifesaver."

"I'm sure she has," he said. "How is Tia?"

Erika responded. "Her leg is broken. It was a compound fracture. Other than that, she has a concussion and some cuts that required stitches. It's amazing that she survived it."

"It was a truck?"

She nodded. "The driver was drunk. At eight o'-clock this morning," she added, unable to keep her anger from her voice.

"But she's going to be okay?" he asked.

"It looks good. We're waiting to hear more from the doctor."

"I just want her to be okay," Brenda said, wringing her hands. "And I hope the insurance on my new job will cover most of the hospital bill." She took a deep breath. "I need a breath of fresh air if you don't mind. I've never liked hospitals. Please let me know if the doctor steps in," she said to Erika, then turned to Gannon. "Nice meeting you. I appreciate you stopping by."

Erika watched the woman leave the room. "I feel for her," she said. "She's trying to cover for her sister in jail and keep her own head above water."

Gannon moved closer to her and slid his hands into his black wool coat pockets. "What about the insurance?"

Erika winced. "The coverage may be iffy because Tia's aunt hasn't been working at this company long."

He paused barely a half beat. "Let me know if there are any gaps in coverage. It will be taken care of."

She stared at him in surprise. "Why? You barely know her."

"But you know her well and she's obviously important to you."

Her stomach dipped and swayed as if she were on a ride at an amusement park. Everything he said and did was indicating that she, Erika, was important to him. "I don't know what to say except thank you."

"Brenda Rogers?" a male voice said.

Erika whipped around to the doctor. "She went outside for just a second. I'll go get her."

Erika raced downstairs to find Tia's aunt just as she was walking inside. She escorted the anxious woman to the waiting room, where Gannon was talking with the doctor.

"Tia is in stable condition," the doctor told Erika and Brenda. "She may need some physical therapy, but after a week or two of rest with moderate daily movement, you'll be amazed at how quickly she recovers. Youth," he said and smiled. "She's groggy from the anesthesia, but I think she'd like a visit."

"Oh, thank God," Brenda said and grabbed Erika's hand. "Will you go with me to see her?"

"Of course." Erika glanced at Gannon.

"Give me a call later," he said.

She nodded, still trying to come to grips with why he had come to the emergency room. She never wanted to overestimate her importance to him. That had been her downfall before.

By the time Erika left the hospital it was midnight and she wasn't feeling anything like Cinderella. Taking a cab, she listened to her voice-mail messages on the way home. Her assistant had left several, and Jessica had called to gently bully Erika about Gerald.

She winced at that message and deleted it. Gannon had left two messages, one from much earlier in the day and one two hours ago instructing her to call him when she went home.

She replayed his messages two times and closed her eyes as she listened to his voice. She had always loved his voice, deep with just a hint of roughness around the edges.

She glanced at her watch again and shook her head. It was after midnight. No way she was going to call Gannon Elliott after midnight.

The following morning she dragged herself out of bed, called the hospital to check on Tia and ingested three cups of coffee. She would have mainlined it if it had been possible. She didn't fight her hair today, deciding to let it go curly as she applied what seemed like half a pot of concealer beneath her eyes.

For the sake of distraction, she rubbed on blush, lip gloss and mascara and wore a red sweater. She hoped it made her appear more alert when all she wanted was another half day of z's.

She rode the train to her office, took off her coat and prepared to sink into her chair.

A knock sounded at her door and Gannon walked into her office. Her heart gave a little bump at the sight of him.

"You didn't call," he said.

"It was after midnight."

He nodded. "You could have called anyway."

"Still awake?" she said in surprise. "I would have loved to have been asleep then. In fact, I think I may have dozed a little on the way to my apartment."

He cracked a half smile. "That sleepy?"

She nodded. "Oh, yeah. This afternoon I may pull out my yoga mat, put a Do Not Disturb sign on my door and take a nap."

"I thought yoga was for meditating."

"In this case meditating on the inside of my eyelids."

He chuckled. "How's Tia?"

"She was a little scared. She tried to put up a brave front for her aunt, and that just ripped out my heart, so I stayed until I talked with the night nurse and Tia conked out."

"You're a good person."

The simple affirmation from him stole all her pithy responses. He was treating her differently and she didn't know how to react. The way he acted could lead her to believe that something deeper than hot sex in his office was going on between them.

She glanced away to get her bearings. "This may sound strange, but Tia inspires me. She comes from this pretty terrible background with her mother being a re-peat drug offender, no father in sight and an aunt who's struggling to keep everything together. But I can tell Tia wants to do better. She's been working like crazy on the article for *HomeStyle*. She's a fighter and she's not afraid to go for it. What's not to admire about that?"

"And maybe you see a little bit of you in her?"

She opened her mouth, then closed it and smiled. "Now, that might be bordering on flattery. I've had quite a few more advantages than Tia has."

"But you've got the fight and the heart."

His gaze was doing strange things to her insides. She looked away again. "Thanks. And thank you also for the offer to cover any insurance problems. That will mean so much to Tia's aunt."

"No problem. What are your plans tonight?"

"Work, then hospital again."

"How long are they keeping her?"

"Another couple of days. I may try to go over to the house and give Brenda a break in the evenings."

He nodded. "Give me a call, and I mean that," he added in a stern voice. "I'll send over my car to take you home."

"That's not necessary," she said. "This isn't really your—" She shrugged. "Your thing."

"It's supposed to snow tonight. Are you going to turn down a ride?"

His gaze was dark with an edge of challenge. What was he trying to do to her? Confuse the hell out of her? Drive her crazy? He was succeeding.

But she absolutely refused to turn down a ride in a toasty car when the weather was horrid and she knew she would be tired.

"Thank you very much," she said.

"You're welcome," he said and left the room, leaving her to wonder.

The next two nights Gannon's car magically appeared to take her home. Erika told herself not to get used to it, but oh, the leather felt nice and the music soothed her. The second night when Carl, the driver, offered her a glass of wine, she accepted it. She talked with Gannon both nights, too.

Since Tia left the hospital on Thursday, he joined her as Erika visited the teen at home. Erika noticed him talking with Brenda while Erika played Scrabble with Tia. Hearing Brenda exclaim, Erika glanced at the two of them and saw Tia's aunt give him a hug.

She asked him about it on the drive home. "What was that about?"

"I just told her she didn't need to worry about the insurance and that I'd arranged for a nurse's aide to help with Tia for the next two weeks."

She shook her head. "When did you decide to get the aide?"

"Hey, I can be generous."

"Yeah, I know. You fund a dozen charities."

"More like nine," he said. "But I have ulterior motives in this situation."

Her heart skipped a beat. "What are those?"

"I'm concerned about your work performance. My dad needs you in top condition to help *Pulse* win my grandfather's challenge."

She blinked. "I haven't been slowing down on my job."

"What about the yoga-mat nap?"

"That was a joke," she said hotly.

He grinned. "I know."

She frowned. "What are you doing?"

"Will you admit you're exhausted doing double duty? Full day at the office. Long evening at the hospital."

She clamped her mouth shut.

"Should have known you wouldn't admit it. Okay, I want Tia taken care of so you can spend some time with me."

His bluntness stole the air from her lungs. She felt as if she were on a rocky ledge, grappling for something to hold on to. "I thought we weren't going to do this again." She glanced away. "We shouldn't have—" She broke off. "In your office, we really shouldn't have—"

His hand covered hers, stopping her rambling. "This is more than sex, Erika. I just want to be with you. Without interruptions. Without ducking and hiding."

She bit her lip. "How? I can't believe you want to date me publicly."

"No," he said. "I don't want to put either of us through the scrutiny." He closed his hand around hers. "Did I ever mention that I have a condo in South Beach?"

"South Beach as in Miami?"

He nodded. "I think we should go down for the weekend."

Her head was starting to spin. "Which weekend?"

"Tomorrow."

"Tomorrow?"

"We can use my private jet."

All she could do was stare at him. This was just too much for her to take in.

He lifted his fingers to her chin. "You said one of your rules was to never turn down a trip to South Florida in the winter."

Erika felt herself pulled in two opposing directions. The beach, warm sun and Gannon Elliott's undivided attention provided an irresistible lure. But she knew this could be one huge, honking mistake, especially if she fell for Gannon again.

The unsigned baby contract was becoming a bigger issue with each passing day. Every time she brought up the subject, he told her that his lawyer would handle it, but since it was such an unusual agreement, it would take time.

Sometimes Erika didn't know which she feared more: running out of time to be with Gannon or facing the prospect of an impersonal sperm donation from a stranger.

Ten

No lines, no intense security inspections, no skimpy snacks or yucky food and no waiting. As Erika looked out the window of Gannon's Cessna, she knew this was one aspect of wealth she could grow to love.

"Just curious," she said to him as he studied a report. "When was the last time you flew on a commercial airline?"

"When I went to Australia two years ago," he said. "No, wait. London, last year. It was a quick trip."

"Those are out of the country. They don't count," she said, knowing there were more perks and better customer service on international flights.

He wrinkled his brow thoughtfully for a moment. "Maybe when I was in college?"

Erika groaned. "You're so spoiled."

His gaze darkening, he shook his head slightly and slid his hand around the back of her neck. He drew her toward him. "Not spoiled enough."

She couldn't help smiling at his playfully dark tone. "Oh, really?"

"Yeah, being with you and not being with you makes me feel—" He broke off as if he were fighting saying the word.

"Cranky?" she offered.

He growled and the sound ruffled her nerve endings pleasurably. "Hungry all the time."

The revelation gave her a little thrill and she smiled. "For me?"

"Yeah, you," he said and lowered his mouth to hers.

Erika sank into the warm, seductive kiss and sighed. She lifted her hands to his shoulders and moved closer. The more miles they left between them and New York, the more she felt herself give in to their temporary escape. She knew all too well that the more she sank under his spell, the more she was going to hurt if and when Gannon lost interest…or changed his mind about her.

The reality poked at her like an annoying price tag left on her clothing. She deliberately brushed the sensation aside. His mouth, his attention, just being with Gannon felt too good.

She pulled back slightly. "Tell me about your condo. Is it near the beach?"

"Not near the beach. *On* a private beach. It's a nice getaway."

"Do you get away much?"

He shook his head. "I bought three of them a few years

ago as an investment. I turned two and kept the penthouse. A couple of my cousins have used it. I stayed in it once during a business trip to Miami. My assistant called to make sure it's stocked with food, wine and beer."

Erika felt a dart of concern. "Does she know who—"

He shook his head. "All she knows is that someone is using my condo in South Beach this weekend, but she doesn't know who. I left a message for my father that I would be back on Monday and that he can reach me on my cell. I made the flight arrangements myself."

"So I just need to make sure that if I get a sunburn, I don't get it on my face, right?"

"Yeah. But I don't want you to get a sunburn anywhere else either."

The way he looked at her told her he had wicked plans for her body. "You know, I've never been to South Beach."

"I plan to show you a good time. Good food, a visit to the bar at Delano's for one of their famous martinis and—"

"And?"

"And maybe I'll turn your head."

As if he hadn't already. As if she wasn't constantly struggling to get her head on straight when she was around him despite the fact that he'd hurt her horribly last year. Add in her crazy but somewhat brilliant idea that he provide sperm for the baby she wanted, and everything about this situation was sideways.

But she was headed for Florida in January with the sexiest, most fascinating man in the universe, and Monday would come soon enough.

Luck was with them. A change in weather brought hot temperatures, although the night turned cool. Gannon's condo oozed a combination of sophistication and comfort, and the view of the ocean nearly made Erika drool. His large balcony boasted chaise lounges ready for sunbathing or just vegging.

Gannon joined her on the balcony. "Get the lead out and change your clothes. It's time for dinner."

"Why should we leave?" she asked, gesturing at the view.

"Because I promised you a good time," he told her and tugged her back inside the condo.

Erika changed into a simple black dress and took along a sweater. Gannon wore a black sweater that emphasized his shoulders and his pecs. Another view that could make her drool, Erika thought.

He took her to dinner at a trendy restaurant that overlooked the activity on Collins Avenue and offered a view of the ocean. Afterward they went to Delano's bar, where they served generous martinis at ridiculous prices. "Now you're spoiling me," she accused. "How am I going to go back to New York in January after this?"

"Don't think about it. That's a rule. No talk about going back until Sunday afternoon."

"That could be dangerous," she muttered. "This whole thing could be dangerous."

"Why?"

She shook her head. "Too hard to explain. Since I have you here, though, I'd like to ask you some questions I didn't have the nerve to ask you when we were involved last year."

"Why couldn't you ask me last year?"

"I was too awed by you. Terrified of offending you."

"No more awe?" he asked with a lifted eyebrow.

"Quit looking for ego strokes. You get them all the time."

"Not from you," he said, dead serious.

As if he needed them from her. Her heart gave a bump. "You blew me away the first time I met you. You still make me..." She searched for words.

"Make you what?"

"Crazy, breathless." She swallowed over a lump in her throat. "Lots of feelings, but don't distract me. I want to know—what does a billionaire wish for?"

"Peace on earth," he said without missing a beat.

She laughed and grabbed his hand, leaning across the table. "Personally, professionally."

He sipped his martini. "The tough questions."

"Uh-huh," she said.

He was silent for a long moment. "I'm not dodging your question—"

"That's good," she interjected.

He tossed her another mocking, dark look. "But I

don't spend that much time thinking about what I want."

"Because you already have it?"

He narrowed his eyes thoughtfully. "I don't spend a lot of time musing. I spend more time doing."

"Well, if you were to muse, what would you want?"

"I haven't thought about it much. I just assume that someday I'll have a family. When my father retires, I'll be promoted into his position if I don't take another position at EPH before that happens."

"Would you like to be CEO of the whole shebang?"

"There's an appeal to having that kind of power," he confessed. "The idea of having that kind of influence over the media is seductive. Think of the impact you could have worldwide."

"Big responsibility, too," she said.

"That's why we check facts five times over on some articles. One wrong slip and four hundred people are killed in a country on the other side of the globe."

"That's one of the things I've always admired about you."

"What?"

"You're harder on yourself than you are on anyone else."

He toyed with her fingers. "Always knew you were a little too sharp."

"You'd rather be with someone not so quick?"

He lifted her fingers to his lips. "You're the one who's here, aren't you?"

"Yeah. So you've told me about your professional dreams. Still haven't said much about your personal dreams except a vague marriage and family…sometime."

"Oh, you're making me think." He groaned. "When I have time to think—and I stay busy enough to make sure that doesn't occur too often—I realize there's never a good time to try to develop a relationship the way I'd like."

Her heart twisted, but she took a breath to keep her voice light. "On the down low?"

He nodded. "But take time to do normal things. Be friends. I have too high a profile to have a normal relationship. I feel like I have to rob Peter to pay Paul."

She pulled her hand from his.

He met her gaze. "I obviously said something wrong."

"It's just that you feel so torn. I don't like being a part of that."

He shrugged. "So you screw up my head some. Yeah, it's true. But being with you makes me feel good. When I'm with you in the office, I have a tough time keeping my hands off you—and I'm not just talking about sex. I want to touch your hand. I want to share an inside joke. If I do that too much, other people will see there's something between us. That could cause problems for you and me. I sure as hell don't want you going back to *HomeStyle*."

"I won't go back to *HomeStyle* as long as you keep

your end of the bargain. Speaking of which, what's happening with the baby contract?" she asked.

He opened his mouth, then closed it. He finished his martini. "Good point. I'll make another call to my attorney first thing on Monday." He waved to a waiter. "Pineapple martini for the lady," he said to the server.

"I haven't finished my first one," she protested.

"Drink up."

"You're not trying to get me loaded, are you?" she asked, unable to keep from smiling.

"No, but I've gone along with your questions. Now you tell me. What does Miss Erika want professionally and personally, besides a baby?"

"I'm building my career to a place where I can have some flexibility."

"The make-yourself-necessary-and-the-company-will-do-anything-to-keep-you philosophy. I'd say you've succeeded at that," he said in a dry tone.

"Gosh, does that mean I should have asked for more money?" she joked.

"Keep going," he said. "What about the TDH?"

"A man. A husband. I would have preferred to do the husband before the baby, but I didn't anticipate any medical issues."

"The medical problem," he said. "Is it that bad?"

She bit her lip. "Bad enough to change my plans. I've even joined an organization for single mothers by choice. But I have to look on the bright side. My friends have already volunteered to be aunties," she confided.

"You told them?"

"Yeah, during a four-martini evening." She winced, remembering the hangover the next day.

"Four?" he echoed. "You've barely finished one."

"Yeah, but these are so big I could swim in them."

"So plying you with liquor is the secret to getting you to loosen your—" he deliberately paused "—tongue."

She laughed at his naughty humor. "Plying me with four martinis is a sure path to a hangover the next morning. That was a crazy night out with the girls."

"Did you tell them about your plan to get me under contract?"

"No," she said with a frown. "They don't even know that you and I were involved. Although they asked a lot of questions last year."

"Why?"

"Because I was sad."

He lifted his thumb to her lip. "No more of that."

Gannon took Erika to a sybaritic club and had no problem dodging photographers since several starlets were more than eager to pose for the camera. It may have been wiser to move their little party back to his condo, but he'd never taken Erika dancing. The two martinis she'd nursed seemed to have lowered her inhibitions, and he wanted to tease a few secrets out of her mouth before he got to her body.

Gannon knew that once he took her back to his

condo he would want to take her straight to bed—and not to sleep.

She laughed as she was pushed against him on the crowded dance floor. "There's nowhere to go," she protested.

"I think it's designed that way so you have to stay close to someone. Make sure it's me," he said, drawing her against him.

He dipped his head and drew in the subtle spicy scent of her perfume. "You smell great."

"So do you," she said. "Your aftershave makes me dizzy."

"It does?" he murmured, sliding his hands over her hips. She undulated against him, making him reconsider his plan to stay at the club a little longer.

She nodded and licked her lips, then pressed her mouth against his. An illicit thrill ran through him.

"I love the way you taste. Love the way you feel. Love the way you think. Most of the time," she added. "Love the way you talk."

"The way I talk?"

"Your voice is very sexy."

He swallowed a smile, wondering if two martinis had been a bit much for her.

She closed her eyes and looped her arms around the back of his neck. "But you're stingy with your heart."

He blinked. "What?"

"Or maybe it's just me. Just when I'm ready to write

you off as heartless, you do something like show up at the hospital the other day." She opened her eyes and met his gaze. "You shouldn't have done that. That kind of thing could make me fall in love with you."

"Ah," he said, thinking that he didn't mind the thought of her being in love with him. Maybe he'd had too many martinis, too.

"That's not a good thing."

"Why not?"

"I did it before and it was horrible when you stopped seeing me." She played with the back of his hair. "I probably shouldn't be here, but you did that nice thing by showing up at the hospital and taking my breath away and making me do crazy things."

"I kinda like being the man to take your breath away and make you do crazy things."

"There are consequences," she told him. "Can you handle the consequences?"

Her expression was so sexy and challenging, it made him so hard that he wondered if he would split the crotch of his slacks. "I think I can."

"Then why are we still in public and not alone in your condo?"

Not needing a second suggestion, he whisked her out of the club and to his condo in no time. As soon as they stepped into the elevator, he took her mouth in a long French kiss that made him sweat.

The way she drew his tongue into her mouth and shimmied against him sent his heart rate skyrocketing.

She slid her fingers into his hair, and the sensation of her touch on his scalp was oddly erotic.

Everything about her was erotic. The way she smelled, the way she moved, the way she tasted. He swallowed an oath and slid his hands up her thighs to cup her bottom, urging her against him to soothe the hard ache she caused.

"You make me—" She never finished the thought as she took his mouth again in an openmouthed kiss that robbed his breath.

He slipped his hands between her thighs, underneath her panties, and found her damp and swollen. It was the sexiest sensation, but he knew there was more.

"I make you what?" he managed.

She gasped as he stroked her.

"So hot," she whispered.

She did the same for him. The elevator dinged the arrival to the penthouse and he urged her through the door.

She tugged at his sweater. He pulled her zipper down and shoved her dress down over her hips along with her little black panties. The urge to be inside her was like a raging fire.

He pulled off his sweater and she unfastened his slacks. He ditched his shoes and slacks and pulled her against him. She wrapped her legs around his waist, her wetness taunting but not enfolding him.

In the back of his mind he remembered protection. For the first time in his life he wavered. She wanted a baby. In a way he'd never wanted before, he wanted to possess her, to mark her as his. An audacious, primitive thought.

He took a deep, not-so-steady breath and put her on the couch. "Back in a second," he whispered.

He grabbed his slacks and the condom inside the pocket and returned to her but made himself wait to look at her. Her hair spilled over the couch with abandon. The stiff peaks of her breasts invited him like cherries on cream. And her thighs were spread open, revealing her swollen femininity.

"You have no idea how sexy you are," he told her. "But I'm going to do my best to show you."

"Another thing I love about you is that you're an overachiever about everything you do."

She made him want to live up to being her overachiever lover. He lowered his mouth to her breasts and inhaled her groans, slid his lips down to her belly button and lower still to take her into his mouth. She arched against him and he decided the taste of her arousal had to be the most addictive thing he'd ever experienced.

"Inside," she whispered. "Inside."

He pulled on the condom and pushed her legs farther apart, plunging inside. She moaned. He groaned.

"Be careful," she told him as he sank into her moist, tight femininity and the deep turbulence of her eyes. "I don't want to love you too much again."

But he was a greedy man. He wanted her. Her body, her mind and her love. And he took everything she offered and gave her more than he'd planned.

Eleven

The trouble with a woman like Erika, Gannon realized after they returned from South Beach, was that being with her was habit-forming. He wasn't sure how she managed to be both comforting and stimulating, but she did it damn well.

Although he'd seen her that morning, his schedule had been too packed to get a chance to talk with her. Then he couldn't turn down his mother's impromptu invitation to a lunch that included his sister and brothers.

Despite his suggestion to make use of the executive dining room, his mother had preferred a café around the corner and indulged in small talk.

"Nice tan," his mother said, smiling as she lifted her brows in silent question.

"Yeah," his sister, Bridget, said. "It must be nice to be able to take time off for a trip to Florida in January."

"You could, too, if you didn't work for the female version of Attila the Hun," Tag said, joking about their hardworking aunt Finola.

"You'll be changing your tune when you report to her as the new CEO," Bridget retorted.

"Remember who your father is," Gannon said, feeling a sharp tug of competitiveness.

"It's just starting," Liam muttered. "We've got an entire year of this."

His mother lifted her hands and shook her head. "No arguments. This was supposed to be a nice lunch for a mother with her children."

"Sorry, Mom," Tag said.

"Back to Gannon's tan," Bridget said. "Take anyone with you?"

Gannon sipped his coffee. "No one I want to discuss."

His mother met his gaze. "Hmm. Must mean you like her if she hasn't shown up in the press."

Karen Elliott might be known for her easygoing nature, but she was shrewd when it came to reading what was going on with her husband and children. Gannon studied her for a moment. He was reluctant to admit to himself that he'd been distracted for most of the meal thinking about Erika, but now that he looked at his mother, he noticed she seemed a little on edge. Her hands were knotted too tightly and at the moment her brows were furrowed.

"What's up with you?"

She pushed her hair behind her ear in a nervous gesture. "Not much. The regular thing. Volunteer work, my reading club, visiting with Maeve." She glanced at her watch. "As a matter of fact, I need to leave for a meeting. But I just wanted to let all of you know that I'm going into the hospital for some tests."

Alarm shot through Gannon. "What?"

"Tests," Tag echoed. "What tests?"

"I don't want to make a big deal about it. It's not unusual to take all kinds of medical tests at my age." Karen was fifty-four.

"But this isn't routine, is it?" Liam asked.

His mother's face looked determinedly neutral. "I've told you as much as I need to."

"But, Mom," Bridget said, "you can't just drop this on us and not explain."

"You would prefer that I not tell you at all?" Karen returned.

Tag cleared his throat. "No. Not at all." He reached to cover his mother's hand. "But you're pretty important to us, so we want to know everything."

She patted his hand and gave a little smile. "Well, all of you are very important to me, too. Now I really should go. Gannon, if you don't mind, could you pay the bill?"

"No problem," he said and stood as Tag helped her with her coat. He leaned toward her and hugged her. "You know you can call me for anything."

"Including grandchildren?"

He groaned. "I should have known you'd find a way to slip that in."

"Don't make me wait forever. 'Bye, darlings," she said and kissed each of them before she left.

Silence fell over the four of them.

"This is weird," Bridget said. "I'm worried."

"She doesn't want us to worry," Liam said.

"What do you think it is?" Tag asked.

"I don't know," Gannon said.

"Has Dad said anything to you?" Tag asked.

"Not a word."

"I don't have a good feeling about this," Bridget said, and from the looks on his brothers' faces and the knot in his own gut, Gannon sensed she was speaking for all of them.

Erika plowed her way through the work that had piled up during her absence on Friday. The afternoon wore into early evening before she took a break and stretched. A light knock sounded on her door and Gannon walked in.

Her heart immediately lifted and she rose from her chair. "It's so good to see you," she said, smiling at the sight of him.

"Same here," he said, tugging her from behind her desk and into his arms. "Are you sure someone didn't try to pack two days into this one?"

"I'm with you on that, but the weekend was great," she said, relishing the feel of his arms around her. "It's like I turn my back and everyone races into my office and dumps their work on me before I can yell stop."

He chuckled. "Oh, this is crazy, but I've missed you."

Her heart tightened at his confession. "I guess we can be crazy together, because I've missed you, too."

He lowered his mouth to hers in a kiss that made her dizzy and warm. She pulled back slightly and looked at him. "That felt like two martinis on an empty stomach."

He gave only a half grin, making her take a second look. Something about him was different. Sure, the office brought the usual pressures, but he seemed more tense.

"What's wrong?"

He narrowed his eyes and glanced away. "Nothing. Regular headaches. Rough landing after my trip to paradise with my dream girl."

Her heart gave a little flip. "I appreciate the flattery."

"It's more than flattery," he told her, his gaze making her heart skitter.

"Thanks," she said, lifting her hand to his jaw. "Dream guy."

His jaw clenched slightly.

She frowned in concern. "Gannon, I don't want to pry, but something's wrong. You can tell me if you want, but you don't have to."

He closed his eyes, inhaling deeply, then exhaling. "My mother is going into the hospital for some tests. She won't tell us what's wrong. Neither will Dad. I grilled him this afternoon and couldn't get anything out of him."

The pain in his voice made her chest hurt. "Oh, Gannon, I'm so sorry. All of you must be sick with worry."

He shook his head. "My father may seem like the

rock of my family—and don't get me wrong, he's solid. But my mother…she's the glue. I mean, look at the personalities in my family. All of us kids have been a handful at one time or another, but she smoothes everything out and makes it work. I don't know what we'd do if something happened to—" He broke off, shaking his head again.

"You can't think that way until you find out the rest of what's going on."

"I prefer having all the information," he said in a rough voice.

"You like having control," she said.

He nodded.

"And you don't have it in this situation."

He sighed. "No. I don't. And I don't understand why she wouldn't confide in her own children."

"Don't you think she must have had her reasons?" she asked.

"She's usually the most reasonable person in the world."

"Then you're going to have to give her some room to do what she feels she needs to do."

"None of us likes being shut out."

"I'm sure you don't. You think she'll tell you more after she gets the test results?"

"Yeah, I just wish I knew…"

"So you could fix it," she added. "What can I do to help you?"

He met her gaze. "You're doing it."

The way he looked at her made her feel light-headed. The way he looked at her made her feel necessary. Was that possible with a man like Gannon?

After that, they spent every night together. It was as if the puzzle pieces between them had clicked together and neither wanted to question it. It just felt right.

Gannon joined her when she visited Tia and he waved coffee under her nose in the mornings to help her wake up. They made love every night and she fell asleep in his arms.

The fact that he still hadn't produced a contract from his personal lawyer bothered her. She'd brought it up several times once he'd insisted it was in its final draft. She had to believe he would come around. Maybe this time she would get the man *and* the baby. Maybe she would get it all.

The prospect made her so breathless she couldn't overthink it.

Gannon joined his family for dinner one of the weekend nights but showed up at her apartment afterward. Erika knew she was falling more deeply in love with him with each passing moment and she couldn't find any motivation to stop herself.

Monday started out the same way. She and Gannon worked their jobs and he surprised her with a rose that evening. Erika carried the secret pleasure of the rose and his attention all through the next day.

Late Tuesday afternoon he entered her office with a

somber expression on his face. He closed the door behind him and adjusted his tie.

Erika felt a spike of alarm. "What's wrong? Is it your mother?"

She rushed toward him, but he held up his hand to stop her. "No. Not my mother."

"Then what is it?"

Shoving his hands in his pockets, he sighed. "The rumors have started again. A copy editor mentioned to an intern that she'd seen us together. It must have been when we took that walk the other night."

She fought a wave of apprehension. "You're not dumping me again," she said.

He shook his head. "No. Not dumping. We just probably need to cool things down for a while."

She didn't find his response at all reassuring. "What do you mean by cool down? And how long is a while?"

"Cool down means we probably shouldn't see each other outside of work for a while."

A knot of ugly tension formed in her throat. "And a while is?"

He shrugged. "I don't know, Erika. Maybe we should put this off until the CEO challenge is over."

She gasped. "But that's a whole year."

His jaw tightened in displeasure. "Yeah, I know. But it might be best."

"For whom?" she demanded.

"For everyone," he said, his impatience bleeding into his voice. "This isn't what I want."

"Well, you sure made the decision fast. I think I was in your bed this morning."

"C'mon, Erika. This is a tough time. My focus has to stay on *Pulse* and getting my father into the CEO position. I have feelings for you, but this isn't the right time."

Feeling like the worst kind of fool, she fought a mix of fury and tears. She felt totally betrayed. He hadn't made promises, she reminded herself, but it didn't matter. She'd allowed herself to believe. She'd let down her guard.

Gannon might watch out for *Pulse,* his father and her job, but he wasn't going to watch out for her heart.

Her throat was so tight she could barely speak. "I don't know what to say. I didn't expect this from you. Again."

"It's not the same thing," he said.

"Yes, it is." She shook her head to clear it. She had to take care of herself. "I can't stay with *Pulse.*"

"What?"

She shook her head again. "I can't stay with *Pulse.*"

"You're not going to use that as a trump card to force me to go public with our relationship, are you?"

He may as well have slapped her. "This isn't about you," she said. "This is about my emotional well-being. Not that you would understand that. I don't want to have to see you every day and—"

"We can make arrangements so we don't have to interact as much," he said.

She shook her head. "No. I don't want to be on the same floor. I'm not going to do that to myself. I'm going back to *HomeStyle* immediately."

"You can't," he said.

"I can. You never signed a contract for me and my contract stipulated that I could return to *HomeStyle* at any time."

He stared at her in disbelief.

An ugly suspicion boiled inside her. "You never even intended to give me your sperm, did you?"

Gannon gave an exasperated sigh. "It was an insane idea. I hoped I could make you see—"

"My insanity," she interjected, fury rising inside her. "Yes, I can and I will return to *HomeStyle*," she repeated, clinging to the resolve growing inside her. "I'm getting off your seesaw, Gannon. And I'm not getting back on."

Gannon stayed up until nearly dawn, prowling his empty, lonely two-story apartment. He could still smell the scent of Erika, hear the echo of her laughter. He didn't want to sit on the sofa because she wasn't there smiling up at him.

As he watched the sun rise over the cold city from his window, he searched his mind for ways to keep her in his life. Sure, he wanted her at *Pulse,* but he wanted her after work even more.

In fact, the want was feeling a lot closer to need. More than sexual, though heaven knew he couldn't get enough of her in bed either.

There had to be a way to negotiate this situation. There was always a way.

Riding the wave of her anger and refusing to give in to her hurt, Erika went to work early and moved her belongings back to her *HomeStyle* office. Her successor hadn't gotten completely settled in, so Erika just stacked her boxes against the wall next to the door.

She left a note for Michael on his assistant's desk simply telling him that she preferred to return to *HomeStyle* because the position suited her better. She arranged a transfer to a highly coveted position for her temporary replacement. No need for the woman to get the shaft just because things hadn't worked out for Erika at *Pulse*.

She kept busy putting her office in order and reacquainting herself with the business of producing *HomeStyle*.

Midmorning an e-mail from Gannon popped up. Even the sight of his name made her heart jump. Disgusted with her reaction, she vacillated over whether to delete it without reading it, but some sick part of her couldn't resist.

He was surprised she'd moved so fast. They should talk about things. A year wasn't so long.

Maybe not for him, she thought and deleted the message.

She told herself she was doing fine—not great but okay—until she walked out of her office and nearly plowed into him. Seeing him shocked the air out of her lungs.

"Hi," he said.

"Hi," she managed.

"We need to talk."

Talking with Gannon got her into trouble. Looking at Gannon got her into trouble.

"I'm busy," she said and was amazed that her feet followed her mental direction to step away from the fire that had burned her twice.

I'm busy became her mantra. She practiced it at odd moments when he invaded her mind. She said it to him when he tried to invade her office. She even began to repeat it in her sleep for the next two nights.

On Wednesday she received an unexpected invitation. Tea on Thursday with Maeve Elliott, the wife of Patrick Elliott, current CEO of Elliott Publication Holdings. Cameras and recorders permitted.

She was so excited she could barely stand it. For months she'd requested an interview with Maeve at the family townhome, but Maeve's assistant had always put her off.

She couldn't believe her luck. What a coup. She immediately began to plan for the meeting, jotting down notes and arranging for a sensitive, polite and talented photographer. She told herself the fact that Maeve was Gannon's grandmother wasn't part of her intense curiosity about the woman. Her interest was purely professional.

Which sounded like bull and she hadn't even said it aloud. The following morning she changed her clothes three times and took an extra outfit to work in case she spilled something on herself.

A half hour before her appointment with Maeve, she and the photographer took a cab to Ninetieth and Amsterdam Avenue. Gannon had told her the place was huge by Manhattan standards, with three stories of living space and an unheard-of half-submerged garage. Erika also knew that Maeve and Patrick's orphaned twin granddaughters lived at the townhome during the week since both of them worked at EPH.

As the cab driver slowed in front of the address, she took in the Manhattan home of Gannon's grandparents. The black wrought-iron gate covered in ivy discouraged uninvited guests. The gray stone building with white trim and a red front door sat back from the street about ten feet.

The photographer, Tom, gave a low whistle. "Nice place."

"It's beautiful. We won't take outside shots in order to protect their privacy."

He nodded in agreement. "I've got my flash ready for inside."

"I'll ask her permission before you shoot," she said, feeling a mixture of excitement and nerves. "Are you ready?"

He nodded and got out of the car, then turned to assist her.

"Thanks," she said. "Great manners. That's part of the reason I chose you."

He smiled. "My mother will be delighted to hear it."

They rang the doorbell and a woman answered the door. "Mrs. Elliott will have tea in the library," she said and led Erika and Tom to the room left of the foyer. The grand entrance boasted a ceiling that went up to the roof and showcased a stained-glass skylight.

Erika spied a grand piano farther down the entryway. She heard the quiet click of Tom's camera as she entered the formal library. The lovely room emanated a warm ambience while filled with antiques.

A silver tray was already set with tea, tiny sandwiches and pastries. Three place settings of delicate rose-covered bone china were placed on the cocktail table.

"I wonder who—"

"Hello, Erika," a familiar voice said from the foyer.

Gannon. She looked at him in surprise. "What are you doing here?" she whispered.

He laughed. "I'm having tea with my grandmother."

Realization sank inside her. "You set this up," she said, unable to keep an accusing tone from her voice.

"Yes, I did. And you're glad I did. Right?"

She opened her mouth and worked it, wanting to stalk out of the town house. But that would have been unbearably rude, and she couldn't give up the opportunity to meet Maeve even with Gannon there.

He turned behind him and extended his hand. "Grandmother Maeve, this is Erika Layven, the managing editor of our new magazine *HomeStyle*."

A small-boned, thin woman with mostly white hair pulled into an elegant updo entered the room. She wore a well-tailored dress and a locket around her neck, but what captured Erika's attention was the spark in her eyes and her kind smile.

"Erika, it's lovely to meet you. Gannon has told me you're a clever, industrious woman with a good heart. He mentioned your involvement in the mentoring program." Maeve extended her hand in welcome as she spoke in her lilting tone.

Erika fought an odd urge to curtsy and shook Maeve's hand instead. "Thank you for inviting me today. I'm honored."

"Please sit so we can enjoy our tea," she said, waving her hand toward the chair across from the settee. "You, too, Gannon. It's been a long time since you took afternoon tea."

Gannon smiled gently at his grandmother. "Can't deny that. I'm usually drinking coffee around this time to get a second wind."

"Tea's better for you," she said and turned to Tom. "Would you like to take a few pictures now?"

"Thank you very much, ma'am," he said and began to snap away.

"May we take a couple with Gannon, too, please?" Erika asked.

Maeve beamed. "I'm always happy to have my picture taken with my handsome grandson."

Gannon threw Erika a questioning glance. "You'll let me see this if you decide to print it."

"Of course," she said, feeling her stomach knot with a sense of loss as she watched him treat his grandmother with such deference. Erika longed to be part of Gannon's whole life, his work, his home and his family. But it would never happen.

Tom took a few more shots and Maeve lifted her hand. "That's enough. I'll ask Annie to bring another setting and you can join us, too."

Tom glanced at Erika with a look of desperation. He was obviously terrified of taking tea with Mrs. Elliott.

"I know Tom would love to stay, but he has another assignment today," Erika said.

"Exactly," he said. "I hope you'll excuse me."

"That's fine," Maeve said. "Don't let us keep you. Be careful with the wind. It's a bit nasty today."

"Thank you, ma'am," he said and smiled, then left for the door.

"What a polite man," Maeve said. "You don't see that often enough these days. Let's have Annie serve the tea and we can chat."

Erika was scrupulously polite during the visit, biting back the urge to scowl at Gannon for ruining the time with his intrusion. She didn't want to be distracted by the way he stretched out his long legs or the way he laughed at his grandmother's tales. She didn't want to notice the deference with which he treated her. She didn't want to think of him as capable of sweet attentiveness. She much preferred the cold-monster image she'd built in her mind as a form of protection.

"Tell Erika how you and Grandfather met," Gannon suggested.

"I was a seamstress in Ireland and he had come for a visit. I was nineteen years old and Patrick was tall with black hair and eyes as blue as the sea. And relentless. When he makes up his mind, there's no changing it," she said, shaking her head. "Back then I had long red hair and a few men wanting my hand, but Patrick just pushed them out of his way. Swept me off my feet and took me away from Ireland, and that was that."

"It sounds like you didn't stand a chance," Erika said.

"Oh I didn't. Patrick, he was already too handsome for his own good. A bit like this one here," she said, pointing to Gannon. "But it was his personality, his will. He had the energy of a summer storm." Maeve smiled. "He still does," she said, her smile fading slightly as she touched the locket hanging around her neck. "We've had our losses, but we have a lot of joy." She glanced at Gannon and squeezed his hand. "It's good to see you. You should take tea more often."

"I should," he said and kissed her cheek. "Thank you for having us."

"I'm always happy to see my grandchildren. And you're right about Erika. Smart and lovely. I can see the good heart," she said.

"Thank you, Mrs. Elliott. This was such an honor and a pleasure."

"I can give you a ride," Gannon said. "My car's waiting."

Erika opened her mouth to protest but didn't want to appear ungrateful in front of Maeve. She bit her tongue. "Thank you."

Maeve led them to the door. As soon as Erika stepped outside, she shot toward the street, feeling a misty moisture in the air that she hoped wasn't a preface to a rainstorm.

"Hey! Wait up," Gannon said, his long stride catching up with hers in no time. "What are you doing?" he asked when she lifted her hand to hail a cab.

"I'm getting a cab."

"I said I'd give you a ride."

"I don't want one from you," she told him, although the misty moisture turned to drizzle.

"Don't be ridiculous. It's almost rush hour. It'll take forever to get a cab and you'll end up paying a fortune."

"I can charge the company," she said, throwing him a dark look. Several taxis passed her by, and getting a taxi in the rain was nearly impossible.

He stood and waited while she waved her hand for several minutes. Frustration ground her down.

"Okay," she grumbled, her tiredness winning. "Thank you. I was going back to the office, but I think I'll just head home."

Gannon opened the door for her and she got in, moving as far to the opposite side of the seat as she could and placing her purse on the seat beside her as a puny barrier.

"I thought you would enjoy meeting Maeve."

She crossed her arms over her chest and stared straight ahead. "I did. Thank you for arranging the visit. I didn't know you were going to be there."

"Would you have turned her down if you'd known I was going to be there?"

"It would have crossed my mind," she muttered.

"But you still would have gone," he said. "Because you've been dying to meet her."

"The meeting gave *HomeStyle* a terrific feature. What's not to like?"

"What did you think of her personally?"

She wished he would stop trying to engage her, but at least he wasn't talking about their relationship. Or lack of it. Erika felt as if a hard rock was lodged in her throat. Every time she breathed it hurt.

"Maeve was lovely and warm. I bet she was always an openly affectionate grandmother."

He nodded. "She was."

"So what happened to you?" She bit her tongue too late. The flip comment flew out of her mouth before she could snatch it back.

Gannon pinned her with his gaze. "Is that a request or a challenge?"

His stormy expression made her a little nervous. "Neither. Forget I said it."

"No. I want you to explain."

"Well, we just don't always get what we want, and it may be hard for you to accept, but that includes you, too."

"Are you saying I'm not affectionate enough for you?"

The interior of the car seemed to close in on her. She became aware of his aftershave and his long legs just inches from hers. She saw one of his hands on his leg and remembered how that hand had felt on her bare skin, how he'd held her and touched her intimately.

She inhaled slowly. "I didn't say you weren't affectionate."

He paused a half beat. "Openly affectionate."

Silence hung between them and her hurt bloomed like a man-eating flower. To be openly affectionate you had to be willing for everyone to know how you felt. Gannon wasn't. After this second go-round, Erika couldn't pretend his insistence for a secret relationship didn't signal a huge lack of commitment.

"Have you missed me?"

"Like a toothache," she said, refusing to let him get at her one more iota.

He gave a rough chuckle. "I miss you," he told her. "I don't want to do without you."

Her heart twisted. "That was your call, not mine."

He took her hand. "All I said was that we needed to cool things down for a while."

Her resentment rose inside her like a bubbling volcano. "Have you successfully cooled off? Has it been that easy for you?"

"No," he said, his eyes changing colors like a turbulent sea. "I'm still burning up for you and I bet you're still burning for me."

He lowered his head and took her mouth in a carnal, possessive kiss that rippled with emotion. She could feel the want and felt an echoing response inside her. With that caress, he ripped aside the fragile construction of her protection against him, and she felt the aching need tear through her like a hurricane out of control.

He pulled back slightly and whispered against her lips. "You still want to be with me. I can taste it."

She pushed against him, upset with herself for giving in so quickly. "Just because I want you doesn't mean I'll be with you. Trust me. I'm used to wanting you and not having you."

Twelve

The crowd roared as the Knicks scored again, putting the home team ahead by six points. Gannon automatically stood, but he couldn't muster much enthusiasm.

Gannon had never lost at anything that was truly important to him, but he was starting to feel as if the wind was turning against him. He had a bad feeling in his gut about his mother's medical tests. His father had seemed distracted the past few days and he still refused to discuss the subject with Gannon.

And there was Erika.

Rather, there wasn't Erika. Every time he thought of her, his chest squeezed so tight he felt as if he were caught in a vise grip.

After he'd given her a ride home following the tea at his grandmother's, he'd called her, but she hadn't picked up her phone or returned his call.

She'd meant it when she'd said no more. She might still have feelings for him, but she'd given up on him.

The reality alarmed him. Unaccustomed to that emotion, he struggled with a sense of emptiness that went deeper than his bones.

He had thought he could reason with her, negotiate, but she was slamming the door in his face every way it could be done.

Damn, he hadn't realized he'd gotten this involved with her. He'd thought he'd been in better control of his emotions than this. He always had before.

Even now, as he sat in prime seats in Madison Square Garden watching the Knicks with his uncle and a few cousins, he felt completely disconnected.

The half-time buzzer sounded and his uncle Daniel nudged him. "You look like you need a beer or two," he said. "We're going to the VIP lounge. Come on."

He opened his mouth to make an excuse, but Daniel interrupted. "No. We're not letting you stay here looking like that."

Gannon reluctantly got to his feet and joined his cousins and uncle for the mob-filled trek to the VIP room. His cousins scattered while Daniel and Gannon nursed beers at a table near the bar.

"You going to tell me what's wrong?" his uncle asked.

Gannon shook his head.

"Then push aside your sadness for the moment and celebrate with me. I've finally found a way to get my estranged leech of a wife to agree to a divorce."

Surprised, Gannon automatically lifted his beer in salute. Everyone in the family knew that Sharon,

Daniel's second wife, had clung to him and everything she could get from being an Elliott despite the fact that Daniel had wanted a divorce for years. "That's great news. How'd you do it?"

"Paid her off. She finally realized there was no way I would reconcile. Word of advice—don't let your father choose your wife. Choose your own. You have to live with her. Your father doesn't."

Daniel's words struck him like a two-by-four. Even though Gannon's father wouldn't dream of choosing wives for his sons, Gannon couldn't help feeling that he was putting off being with the woman who made him feel happier than he'd ever been because of his grandfather's aversion to scandal and the recent CEO challenge.

Daniel paused midgulp, studying Gannon. "You look like you just took a right hook to the jaw."

"Close," Gannon said, a dozen emotions churning inside him.

Daniel narrowed his eyes. "I'm not the most intuitive guy on the block, but this is looking like a woman problem."

Not bothering to deny it, Gannon nodded.

"I haven't seen you take much of a fall for any woman," Daniel said, then gave a rough chuckle. "I guess it's your turn."

"It sure is bad timing," Gannon said, shaking his head.

"It's almost always bad timing. Bad timing is easier to deal with than the wrong woman, though. Trust me."

Gannon took another long swallow. "What are you saying?"

"Despite the fact that I'm facing my second divorce—or maybe because of it—my advice is simple. If you find a woman who makes you whole, do whatever it takes to get her and hold on tight."

At five after ten on Tuesday morning a dozen beautiful red roses blooming with fragrance arrived at Erika's office. There was no card attached.

Erika felt a sinking suspicion Gannon had sent the flowers. The absence of a card was consistent with his goal to stay under public radar.

The notion filled her mouth with a bitter taste and she considered tossing the arrangement out the window. But the roses were so pretty and smelled so lovely.

She could pretend anyone had sent them.

A second bouquet of roses arrived at ten-thirty. Again no card.

A third bouquet arrived at eleven. No card. A fourth at eleven-thirty. A fifth at noon.

Erika began to feel self-conscious. Her office smelled like a florist's shop, and coworkers knocked on her door to see the arrangements placed on every available surface.

Another dozen roses arrived at twelve-thirty. Furious that Gannon had made a spectacle of her, Erika dialed his extension. When his assistant picked up, she demanded to speak to him.

"I'm sorry. He's on another line right now. I'll give him the message that you called."

A knock sounded on the door and Erika ground her teeth and hung up the phone. Her assistant, Cammie, peeked inside, her face lit with excitement. "More roses!" she said and brought in yet another bouquet.

Erika swore under her breath. "I want these taken to the hospital."

Her assistant gaped at her. "What? But you can't. They're for you. And they're beautiful."

"And I have too many," Erika said. The flowers made her nervous. Red roses signified love, the long-lasting kind, and being surrounded by all these American Beauties underlined the fact that Gannon didn't love her the way she loved him. "Call the closest hospital and ask if there are four people who could use some roses to cheer them up."

Her assistant looked crushed. She sighed. "Okay. If you really want me to."

"I really want you to," Erika said firmly and closed the door after her assistant left.

Seconds later another knock sounded at her door. Her temper ratcheted up another notch. Another interruption. Probably another coworker wanting a look at her office full of roses. She jerked open the door. "This is not the company sideshow provided for your viewing entertain—" She broke off when she saw Gannon with a man she didn't recognize by his side, along with his assistant and hers.

They were all staring at her.

She cleared her throat, embarrassed and more rattled than she could recall. If it had just been Gannon, she would have verbally scalded his gorgeous self. But there were others. She was forced to save her blasting of him for later. "Is there something I can help you with?"

"Yes, there is," he said, his gaze deadly confident.

Erika's nervousness intensified. That expression of his had always foreshadowed trouble for her. Big trouble. "I'm busy this afternoon, but—"

"This will just take a few minutes," he said and led his troops into her space. "Nice roses."

"Beautiful," she said. "But a little overdone considering there was no card. Anonymity requires less courage, don't you think?"

His lips twitched slightly. "I agree. That's why I brought along my personal attorney, Harold Nussbaum, and my assistant, Lena, and yours. I wanted witnesses."

Confusion raced through her and she swallowed an oath. Had he changed his mind about the insemination? And was he going to let the whole office in on it? She glanced past him to the open door.

"Should we close the door?" she asked.

He shook his head. "The more, the merrier." He moved closer to Erika, his gaze purposeful.

Her heart rate picked up.

"I'm here to tell you in front of witnesses that I love you."

Her assistant, Cammie, gave an audible gasp.

Erika's heart shot into her throat. She stared at him in shock.

"You make me laugh. You make me think. You make me feel more than I ever thought I could. I want to be with you all the time. I want the chance to love you forever. I think you're better at this loving thing than I am, but if you're patient with me, I know I can learn."

A well of emotion expanded in her chest, making it impossible for her to breathe. Was she hearing things? Was this really happening?

He got down on one knee and she felt light-headed. She had to be dreaming.

He extended his hand toward her, waiting for her to reciprocate with her own hand, but all she could do was stare.

"Give him your hand," her assistant whispered.

Erika tentatively slid her now ice-cold fingers onto his warm palm. His hand enclosed hers and she met his gaze, swallowing over the lump of emotion in her throat.

"I love you. I want us to be together always. Will you marry me?"

She met his gaze and could have sworn all the clocks in the world stopped. But she was still afraid. Was she having a monster delusion? "Could you please repeat the question?"

She heard his assistant give a nervous giggle.

"I said, will you marry me?"

"Are you sure you want this?" she asked, ignoring everyone but Gannon.

"More sure than I've ever been about anything."

"Why? Why are you so sure?"

"Because I've found the woman of my dreams—you. And I don't want to waste one more minute of my life without you."

His words filled her like a warm breeze. His hand holding hers and the commitment in his gaze told her she wasn't having a delusion. He was real and so was his love for her.

Her eyes burned with a sudden infusion of moisture. "I feel like I've been waiting for you forever."

"Thanks for letting me catch up," he said. "Will you?"

She nodded. "Yes, yes, yes."

His assistant and hers made sniffling sounds as he rose to his feet and took her in his arms.

"This was lots better than any card you could have sent with the roses," she said. "But you didn't have to bring witnesses."

"I didn't?" He held her tight against him, making her feel cherished.

"No, but I'm glad you did. If I'm afraid I dreamed it, I have someone to call."

"You won't need to call anyone," he said and pulled a black velvet jeweler's box from his pocket. He flipped it open to reveal a huge diamond ring, then he lifted her hand to put it on her finger.

"That stone is ridiculously large," she murmured.

"I wanted you to have a tangible reminder of this day."

She was so full of joy and amazement and love. "I want you to be my tangible reminder."

"Oh, sweetheart, you can count on it," he said and took her mouth in a kiss. A crowd of coworkers craned to see inside, but Erika didn't care if anyone else saw what she and Gannon had going on. The most important person in the world had just told her that he loved her. Nobody could top that.

A crazy question nudged at her. "Which magazine will I work for? *Pulse* or *HomeStyle*?"

"Whichever one you want. As long as you remember that you and I will be working on making a baby every night," he whispered.

Erika felt every cell in her body smile. "Something tells me you won't let me forget."

* * * * *

Don't miss the next installment of
THE ELLIOTTS.
Be sure to pick up
TAKING CARE OF BUSINESS
by Brenda Jackson,
available in February from Silhouette Desire.

WHAT HAPPENS IN VEGAS...

Shock! Proud casino owner
Hayden MacKenzie's former fiancée,
who had left him at the altar for a cool
one million dollars, was back in Sin City.
It was time for the lovely Shelby Paxton
to pay in full—starting with the wedding
night they never had....

His Wedding-Night Wager

by **Katherine Garbera**

On sale February 2006 (SD #1708)

Also look for:

Her High-Stakes Affair, March 2006
Their Million-Dollar Night, April 2006